The Millionairist
JANETTE RUCKER

The Millionairist

Janette Rucker

To order additional copies of this book, contact:
Lighthouse Literary
100 NE 5th St, Oklahoma City,
OK 73104, USA
support@lighthouseliterary.us
(405) 339-0577

CONTENTS

TABLE of CONTENTS

I would like to thank God first, then my parents Robert and Janette Andrews, next my siblings Earl, Micheal Jerry and Linda my aunts and uncles, nieces, nephews, sister-in-laws and brother-in-law and my cousins and my best friends Benita Andrews, Vernal (Itsy) Gibson and Wanda Dixon and Vivian Taylor, love you Ladies. More thanks to my church family. Special shout outs to Tia Andrews Sara Stewart and Rosie Lester for helping me type my books. Special thanks for my nephew Bendrea Andrews for making the covers much love Dre and also thanks to my friends and last but not least my husband Robert Rucker. I love you baby. JAR.

FROM THE AUTHOR

First I'd like to give thanks to God for the will and the strength, time and patience to write another book. This one came from deep inside and I'm hoping that everyone that reads this will be, entertained by this book. And also enlightened by some of the messages I tried to weave into this tale. One was how Diamond/Diane found out that the business made her a millionairist, but having her family made her complete and it's priceless. She learned she couldn't put a price tag on a loving family. It is my wish; some people will get what I was trying to get across and to my husband Robert, my back bone and me being his rib that God took out. I thank you and I love you for allowing me to get my feelings out by writing this book.

GOD BLESS YOU ALL

Janette "Carol" Rucker

9-20-07

THE MILLIONAIRIST

This story is about a young black woman who came from rags to riches left an infant to a strong struggling black family that had a lot of love but not much money. Diamond's birth mother Lillie a young girl with trials of her own living in a nightmare of an abusive mother who decided Lillie was the reason of her unhappy life made her life hell but no way was Lillie going to make her daughter live through her horror so she gave Diamond a chance to live by giving her up. Diamond went from the garbage can to the mansion but still trying to find genuine love from a man that could deal with a successful black woman without his hands always in her pocket but his mind on her heart.

PROLOGUE

Later as Quenton and the girls entered the house it was an unfamiliar smell in the house, cooked food. As they looked around the house it was clean some things were moved around and "Diane" was in the kitchen cooking. Quenton looked up and pointed up and said "Thank you!" because he knew God had brought this woman to him. The girls were looking around happy because their room's was clean. Diamond even washed the clothes. After eating a great meal of roast beef, potatoes and vegetables everyone left the table full and the girls went to help "Diane" with the dishes. Quenton went and called his father Ray. "Hello." Ray said. "Daddy, she can cook!" Quenton yelled happily. "Well then, the next phone call you make had better be to a Preacher, boy don't let her get away."

"She's beautiful sweet, can cook, clean and she gave me her love what more can a man ask for" Quenton thought, until he walked into the kitchen and saw "Diane" and his two girls laughing and washing dishes together. Watching his babies happy and bonding with this wonderful woman made him go to his room and shed a few tears. Quenton was a strong man and after so long trying to get his home together being the daddy, but those girls needed a mama and he had found her.

CHAPTER 1
Alley Way

It was a cold, dark night in a small town in Oregon. Lillie Morgan walked through the long alley and struggled with the pain that raked her body. The baby inside her was fighting to get out. Lillie at age fifteen years old was scared her small body caring the weigh of this baby and not having anyone to go to for help. Remembering back to the moment she woke up out of the small bed she slept on. Soak from her water that broke. Lillie put on a big tent dress, the one she wore a lot lately to hide her pregnancy from her mother Josie. Who was a young mother herself at thirty she felt Lillie was to blame for all her troubles. Josie told Lillie that she shouldn't of had delivered her, but that did not stop her from having five additional children.

Lillie a small framed girl with light skin and brown eyes always wore her hair in a long braid. She was a shy, quiet girl, who at fifteen didn't have any friends and wasn't allowed to go to school. Lillie had responsibilities, she had to stay home and watch her younger sisters and brothers. Lillie had no social life . . . So how could she end up pregnant? She knew people would ask. Lillie thought she should have gone to the hospital. She knew if she went her mother would find out and would be angry at her. She didn't want that, she figured she messed up her mother's life enough; she couldn't bring anymore trouble to her.

As Lillie walked through the alley a pain hit her so hard she backed up to the side of an old building. She pressed her back hard against the building taking the pressure off her feet slowly she slid down the wall to the ground. Sitting on the cold concrete the pains came more frequently. Lillie heard a noise; she looked across the alley and saw a big rat looking at her like she was an uninvited guest at his house. Lillie looked around and saw an empty beer bottle. She reached for it, grabbed it and threw it at the rodent and it ran away; Lillie was relieved because she wasn't able to get up and run. As she sat there wondering what she was going to do next, she thought about how she got to this point.

As a young girl of five, she had a sister named Rainy who was three and a baby brother named Billy. They all lived in a nice big home with their Grandmother Dorothy Morgan. She was a full figured middle age woman with brown skin, short hair that she would always have styled up, when she wasn't wearing one of her big pretty church hat on Sundays. Dorothy was a Christian woman who had two daughters, Teresa who was eighteen and just getting out of high school and getting ready for college. Teresa was a medium framed woman. She wore her hair in a long weave. Teresa had brown skin and was beautiful as well as smart. Then there was Josie, Lillie's mother. Josie was twenty years old, and was like her sister brown skin with a drop dead figure. She had naturally long hair, she was beautiful, but she wasn't very smart Josie dropped out of school early after getting pregnant with Lillie, then Rainy came and then Billy. Dorothy was trying to help her daughter, but she was getting tired. She felt she had raised her daughters and they both were grown now and she wanted to live her life. Her husband their father had died ten years back and now she was ready to start dating again. Dorothy was only forty years old and still in her prime but now her daughter Josie was messing up her plans. Dorothy loved her grandchildren, but this was not what she looked forward to in her later years to keep raising kids. What made matters worst was the fact that Josie didn't stop at one she brought two more.

One night Lillie over heard her mother and her Sister Teresa arguing. "Why don't you keep your legs closed! Mama can't keep taking care of all those babies you keep bringing home!" "Teresa Yelled!" "Mine yo business, you just mad cause you can't get no man!" Josie yelled back. Teresa stopped, looked at her sister who she knew just didn't get it and told her sister, "Josie you got three kids, you didn't finish school, you're out all night leaving the kids for me or mama to watch. When you are here you don't even take care of them then. You're drunk you smell like sex and then you go to bed wake up and do it again! You need to wake up, because we're all getting tired of your shit!" "So what are you going to do about it Teresa! This ain't your house. Why don't you just leave and give us another room!" Josie said and walked out of the house. She didn't come back for two days. Lillie listen as Aunt Teresa would talk to her mother and tell her that she has to put Josie out. Dorothy would always say she couldn't do that but then little Danny came two years later. Then after Josie had Keith that was it for Dorothy she had to kick her out, she hated to do it, but she wasn't going to put her life on hold as Josie kept running the streets and dropping babies off for her to raise. "Why you putting us out where we gonna live, those are your grandchildren and you gonna just put them out on the streets what about me, I'm your daughter!" Josie cried. "I tried baby, but I can't do this anymore, if you're grown enough to keep having kids then your grown enough to start taking care of them." So Josie moved out, she and her five children moved in this poor section of the town into a small three-bedroom house. Josie had a friend of hers help her get on welfare and get food stamps. Josie was upset, she was living in this old house instead of that big beautiful house, her mother had. It had five bedrooms and a full and completed basement with a huge backyard and now she was cramped into this shack with all these kids.

CHAPTER 2
Mama Drama

Josie thought about her life and how she wanted to be a fashion model. When she was a freshman in school. She was a cheerleader and very popular and very excited when the quarterback on the varsity football team chose her. Josie thought she was all that. When she went to the prom with him she felt so special hanging with him. When he asked her to go all the way with him, her first thought was NO, but then she didn't want to lose him because he told her if she didn't he would find someone else that would so she did. Nine months later here came Lillie. Josie had already dropped out of school when her so-called boyfriend went out of state to college. His family made sure that she knew the baby was her problem. After that Josie gave up. She had a baby, no man, no school, and no future. It was then she felt, in her mind that it was Lillie who ruined her life. Lillie was never shown any love: no hugs or kisses, only yelling, cursing and hitting. Early in her life Lillie went through this abuse day in and day out.

After moving to the small house with Josie, Lillie shut down. She had no spirit. She would only talk in whispers afraid she would say something wrong and be slapped. Lillie always hung her head low and wouldn't look anybody in their eyes, in fear of being hurt her Grand mama and Aunt Teresa were the only ones that were nice to her and her sibling. They would take them to church, parks and even out to eat. At Dorothy's house the children had food and clothes, but when they moved in that house with Josie they went without. Josie would take the food stamps and only give Lillie half to buy food. Lillie was only twelve at the time but she had to buy the food, clean the house, and wash what little clothes they had, it was terrible. They wouldn't have a lot to eat and sometime Lillie didn't get to eat at all. She was skin and bones. Josie would sleep all day then get up at night, then she would go out and bring strange men home. Lillie's job was to keep the children in their room and keep them quiet. Lillie was a slave and Josie worked her and made her life horrible. Josie felt Lillie ruined her life, so Lillie was going to stay home and take care of hers. That's why Josie didn't allow

Lillie to go to school. Josie told the people at the school that Lillie was mentally retarded and because Lillie wouldn't speak up, they believed her. Lillie remembered how she would try to stretch the food stamps as far as she could; but there were five of them. Josie usually never ate at home and she did the same at her mother's: sleep all day, and be gone at night. Only this time she could bring men home. She couldn't at her mama's house. Josie was so messed up. She had so many men in her life to the point she didn't really know who the father of her last three children was. Josie thought she was using them by getting their money, but couldn't see she was the one being used. She always had to have a man in her life to keep her hair and nails done and with the latest clothes and the most stylish tightest outfits. When she went out at night to the clubs or casinos, she was always looking good. If she didn't come with a man she surly was going to leave with one. Josie spent their money and when she ran out of theirs, she spent any other money she could get. Even if it meant selling her food stamps leaving only a small amount for the house. Most of the time the little bit she left didn't go very far.

One occasion while Lillie fixed the plates, her sister and three brothers, sat at the table in their small kitchen. Lillie laid out five plates, and was able to give the kids each one drumstick, three spoons full of corn and a few pieces of fried potatoes. Lillie had only a few potatoes on her plate and there was no meat left. The other kids looked at her with sad eyes knowing this wasn't going to fill them up; they would go to bed hungry for another night. Before anyone could eat, they heard a knock on the door. Lillie knew not to let anyone in when Josie wasn't home. With a whisper Lillie asked who it was. Dorothy said, "This is Grandma and Aunt Teresa, open the door." After they came in bringing toys for the children Dorothy said, how she missed all of them. Josie hadn't called or stopped by in weeks. Usually Josie would visit and tell her mother how the kids were doing in school. Then Teresa went around and hugged all the kids that sat at the table. When she saw the plates sitting in front of each child she was shocked. She asked Lillie was that all they had to eat. Dorothy looked at the plates and started to get misty eyed. She looked in the refrigerator and cupboards. There was no food anywhere aside from a few crackers. Both ladies looked at each other in shame. Dorothy was a well to do Christian woman whose husband had left her well off. Teresa was a top associate in an investment firm; she owned a condo, an expensive car and clothes. She was single with no kids and had money put-up and for her and her mother to see their family sitting at the table with only scraps to eat and wearing clothes that were old and torn that looked like they were handed down to each other. Teresa couldn't believe they looked so bad and Lillie looked the worst. Lillie was skinny wearing an oversized dress and sad looking. Teresa noticed Lillie's hung head and lack of eye contact. They never knew the reason for her behavior was because when they weren't around they didn't see how many times Lillie got slapped or put down by Josie. Josie knew her mother and her sister would not allow her to treat Lillie that way, but when they weren't around all of the children were cursed at or hit. Lillie always received the largest doses of Josie's rage and frustration. Lillie always thought it was her fault and loved and had sympathy for her mother more than anybody in the world. All she wanted to do is see her mother smile at her, she would love a hug or even a kiss, but if she could just get a smile from her she would be okay with that. The only time Josie would smile or laugh was when she came home drunk or with a man, but Lillie wasn't giving up, she was going to make her mother happy. She vowed she was going to be there for her mother no matter what, even if it meant staying with her the rest of her life. Later Dorothy told Lillie and Teresa to come in the other room; then she asked Lillie what was going on. Why didn't they have food? Where was Josie? And why didn't she leave a number so they could reach her? What about the clothes the kids had on?

Dorothy was really upset a few months ago she gave Josie money to buy new clothes for the kids. After looking around she didn't see any of her money put to that use. Dorothy was boiling mad, but that was nothing compared to the way Teresa was looking. "Mama, when that tramp walk her ass in this house, I'm gonna beat her down!" Teresa said angrily. "I know how you feel I can't believe Josie could be so heartless. I'm gonna have to take these kids back before someone calls child services on her." Dorothy said with disappointment in her voice. Hours went by, Dorothy and Teresa went to the store and bought a bunch of groceries. They filled the cupboards and the refrigerator, and bought the kids new clothes and shoes. They ordered pizza and sat with the kids to eat. The children felt like it was Christmas. Dorothy was feeling good seeing the kids happy, all of them but Lillie. It was hard to tell whether she was happy or not because she never smiled at all. When the children stayed with Dorothy she would take them all to church; that's the only thing Lillie took an interest in. Dorothy knew the kids wanted to go home and live with her, but there were so many of them. The youngest ones would need babysitters and she knew Lillie would never leave her mother. After Teresa and Dorothy put the children to bed each of them stayed up waiting for Josie to come home. It was 3:00AM when Josie walked in the door. With Josie was a man who looked about sixty and both of them were falling over drunk. Teresa jumped up and grabbed Josie by the hair and threw her against the wall. Dorothy told the drunken man to get the hell out of her daughter's house before she called the cops. Then Dorothy push the man out the door and slammed it. She waited next to the door while Teresa slapped some sense into Josie. Josie was trying to fight back but was too drunk to truly defend herself. Dorothy allowed this to go on until she felt Josie had had enough then Dorothy pulled Teresa off Josie to break it up. Teresa yelled angrily "Let me get her!" Dorothy was now standing between them trying to keep them apart. Dorothy was torn on one hand she wanted to slap the hell out of Josie and take the children home with her. The only problem with that was she knew if she took the children Josie would come back because she wouldn't have any income and she'd probably have another baby. Dorothy was enjoying her freedom to come and go when she pleased. She had a gentleman friend she was seeing; she was in lodges and a member of several different clubs, and a leader in her church. Dorothy wasn't ready to give all of that up to take care of babies again. "What's wrong with you Josie? I never left you and your sister at home by yourselves late at night. You always had food and clothes. How can you do your kids this way? And poor Lillie, she looks like she's just wasting away; what is she so scared of she barely opens her mouth. What have you done to her?" Dorothy asked. "Mama you and Teresa can't come up in my house trying to tell me what to do. This is my house! And unless you want to take care of all these brats I suggest you butt out, cause I know both of you are on your high horses thinking you're all that; living in a rich high class life and don't want none of this. And about Lillie, if I wouldn't of had her in the first place I wouldn't be in this situation now. I could have been a top model, maybe met a rich man to be with. Instead of being in this Hell Hole!" Josie yelled back. Then Josie looked around the room and saw Lillie standing in the corner tears running down her face. Teresa spotted Lillie and said "Josie you act like these kids asked to be here. You're the one who couldn't keep your legs closed. Ain't you heard of Aids? You lucky you didn't get it. But you do have these children. And look how you're hurting this girl!" Josie just turned her head and rolled her eyes.

Dorothy was filled with anger, grabbed Josie and looked into her eyes. "I've had enough of this from you. I'm giving you one more chance to be a mother to these kids. The next time I come over here there better be food in this house and these kids better have decent clean clothes on their backs or so help me! I'll call child services myself!" After Dorothy and Teresa left Josie went over to Lillie and grabbed her face and got eye to eye with her. "I told you don't let anyone in this house when I'm gone. I don't care who it is. You always causing problems for me!" she screamed. Lillie spoke in a whisper; "I'm sorry mama." "No you ain't sorry! But you will be!" Josie shouted, then staggered to bed. Lillie wiped her eyes and went to the room she shared with her sister. She laid on her pallet on the floor and told herself she had to stop making her mother unhappy.

* * *

A year later Josie had another child; a baby girl she named Cindy. Now there were six children in the house. Josie was afraid of what her mother would say and knew if child services took the kids; she wouldn't have any money or a place to stay. Josie stop selling the food stamps so Lillie was able buy groceries to feed her brothers and sisters. Lillie only thirteen had to take care of her baby sister like Grandma Dorothy had to for them. Josie would have the child then leave the responsibility of caring for them to someone else. Lillie loved her baby sister; she fed her, changed her, and rocked her. This was Lillie's way of trying to get her mother to love her. Rainy, Lillie's other sister was not having it. She was like her mother; she only cared for herself. She wouldn't help Lillie do anything. Rainy and Josie would argue and yell at each other all the time. Josie and Rainy's fighting got to the point where Rainy couldn't take it anymore and left to stay with Dorothy. This left Lillie, her three brothers and her baby sister. Josie was happy Rainy left, she was too much drama. Lillie did what she was told and the boys were easy: as long as they were fed they were happy. Josie continued to go out partying all night, sleep all day until Josie met Randy Adams.

Randy was a thirty two-year-old playboy. He was a big-time drug dealer who was tall light skinned with wavy black hair, smooth skin and a nice tight body. He was new in town. He drove a black Mercedes Benz and lived in an expensive condo. Randy would come to the club and spend lots of money. All the ladies were trying to get at him, including Josie. Then the night came when Josie was out at the club sitting at a table with her friends. That's when Randy sent a drink over to her. She looked over at him and he gave her a wink. Josie smiled back at him and watched him all night and when he got up to the door to leave, Josie was right behind him. Josie told him she needed to pay him back for the drink he bought her giving him a sexy smile. Josie left with Randy and stayed with him for the next two days.

As she woke up lying in a king size bed, in this huge condo with all the furnishings of a show place, next to this fine brother. For once she thought things were going to happen for her. She dreamed of being married to this brother. When Randy woke up he told her he had to take care of some business; so unfortunately for Josie she had to go home. Randy sent Josie back to the ghetto in a cab. When she walked in the house Lillie was sitting on the couch with her baby sister laying next her. Lillie's eyes lit up when she saw her mother. She was so happy because she had been worried. Lillie jumped up to embrace her mama, but Josie put her arms out to keep Lillie from hugging her. Lillie backed away and watched Josie walk to her room and close the door behind her. All Josie could think of was Randy. She kept going to the club hoping she could see him again. A few days later Randy came walking in. He sat down at the bar Josie sat across the room looking at his back, hoping he would come over to talk to her. When he didn't, she approached him. As Josie left, her girl friends were laughing behind her back saying how stupid she was to think any man would want a woman with six babies. Randy was sitting at the bar talking to another woman when Josie walked up. He was amused at how Josie made the other lady leave by sitting next to him and striking up a conversation like the other lady wasn't even there. Randy and Josie talked a while then ended up in his condo in his bed for yet another excursion.

"So why don't you talk about your life, your home, your family?" Randy asked the next day over their steak and lobster dinner on his marble dining room table. Josie thought about it and knew she would run him off if she told him the truth, so she lied. She told him she was working part time as a model. She figured once she got him hooked; if he learned the truth it wouldn't matter, plus if he wanted to leave, she would go with him. She would leave everything and maybe he'd never have to know. Randy and Josie continually to see each other Josie would go home sad when she had to leave Randy, but happy she was going to see him again. Lillie notice that her mother was changing, she wasn't yelling or cursing. Josie felt like a new woman she was so in love with Randy that she left all the other men. Lillie liked waking up and not seeing strange men walking through their home.

Life was getting better until one night, Lillie and the kids were sitting doing their normal routine. Josie was in her room doing what she normally did sleeping when they heard a knock on the door. Lillie knew better than to open the door, so she sat and stared at it. The person knocked a few more times. Josie came out of her room and went to the door and opened it. Standing on the other side of the door was Randy. Josie mouth fell open, tears started coming from her eyes. Randy stuck his head through the door and saw all the kids, sitting in the living room then he looked at Josie. "They told me you were just a bitch with a whole bunch of babies. They said they all got different daddies. But you know what, I couldn't believe it. I had to see it for myself. What were you trying to do, Make me your next baby daddy or worst all these kids daddy that you had. I think not. Forget my number!" Randy turned around and walked away. Josie stood watching him leave until she blew up in anger and started yelling and cursing the kids out. All the kids were confused and wondering what they did wrong. The younger ones were in tears. Josie told them all to go to their room. Lillie was hurting for herself but mostly for her mother, went to her room, put baby Cindy to bed and prayed for happiness for her mama.

Things got worst after Randy left Josie she got even meaner to the kids. Every time they saw her she was bringing men home. So many different men wondered into Josie's bedroom late at night. Almost every night strange, drunk, and high men fumbled around the house. Lillie tried to stay in her room when her mama had company but one night when she got up to go to the kitchen to get a bottle for Cindy, who was in her cradle in the room Lillie bumped into a strange man coming out of her mother's bedroom. The door was open in Lillie could see Josie laying in her bed passed out drunk. The strange man looked at Lillie and grinned at her. He smelled of alcohol, Lillie was scared he kept looking at her and walking toward her. Until he got close enough to grab her. "Yo mama passed out without taking care of me. So you gonna have too little girl," he slurred. Lillie tried to pull away but the more she jerked the tighter he held her. The man yanked her down into the basement then pushed her to the ground. He jumped on top of her and put his hand over her mouth and raped her. Lillie tried to yell for her mama through his hand. He then just slammed her head to the ground. She didn't know what hurt worst, the pain to her head or to her private area. As she laid there, she remembered the man telling her before he left, "If you tell your mother I'm coming back to get both of you." Lillie now thinking of her mama and not wanting her to be hurt she knew she had to suffer this terrible ordeal by herself. Lillie washed the blood off the floor, no longer a virgin, took a shower and got in bed. The next day as she watched her mother walk out the house again like always not saying anything-like where she was going, when she was coming back, Lillie wanted to tell her mother what happened. She was hurting and needed someone Lillie wanted her mother to hug her and make it feel better.

Months went by, Lillie was throwing up and sick every morning. She hadn't had a period in months, she was quiet and shy, but she wasn't stupid. She saw her mother go through this enough to know she was pregnant. As her brothers went to school, Josie was in bed sleep and baby Cindy was curled up in her cradle in Lillie's room. Lillie thought to call her grandmother or her aunt. But she knew better, because if she would have called them they would call child protective services, and they would all be taken away from their mother and that couldn't happen. So the time went on and Lillie got further a long. She hid her pregnancy well. Lillie wore big baggy clothes and stayed in her room as much as possible. Her mother was always sleeping or out in the streets. She rarely noticed the kids. Josie wanted Lillie to take care of everything. Things got harder as Lillie got to her last month. And it was hard hiding from Dorothy. Lillie did what ever she could to avoid her she would say she was sick or stay in her room. Until the night came when Lillie found herself now in the alley ready to deliver her own child.

CHAPTER 3

Diamond in the Rough

Lillie laid in that alley, pains hitting her harder and harder. She screamed, she moaned, she cried until finally, with one big push the baby introduced herself to the world. Lillie looked down at this baby girl she was beautiful. Lillie took her sweater and wiped her off as much as she could and with all her strength she pulled herself up. With her baby in her arms she struggled along through the alley until she reached a small house. Inside she could see a black man and woman and two kids sitting at their dinner table. This was the family the baby needed. Lillie staggered to the back of the house and laid the baby on top of the covered garbage can. It was cold and dark but she knew what she had to do. In her soft voice she told her baby, "I don't know you, but I already love you too much to bring you pain like I've been going through. Have a good life." Lillie kissed her child. She walked to the back door and knocked on it then hid behind the great big tree. She waited until this short, dark, full figured woman opened the door. She scanned the backyard looking for whoever knocked on the door, until she saw a bundle laying on her garbage can. Immediately she called for her husband, "Oh my God Curtis come see!" "What's wrong Beulah," the tall, dark, heavyset man said. He stood in shocked, rubbing his eyes in disbelief. Beulah picked the baby up and looked at her. She told Curtis they had to go to the hospital right away. The couple took their kids next door to a neighbor, got in their car and drove off. Lillie walked slowly, and painfully home.

Once Lillie made it in the house she fell on the floor and just laid there. She laid there until one of her little brothers had to go to the bathroom when he saw all the blood on the floor he ran to wake up his mother.

Josie was upset she didn't like being disturbed. She got up and saw Lillie and the blood all over the floor. Josie was scared she picked Lillie up and placed her in the backseat of her beat up Volvo some man gave her and rushed her to the hospital. Josie was yelling at Lillie all the way there. Josie screamed about how much trouble Lillie was. She was cursing because she had to leave Billy who was only eleven at the house to watch the rest of the kids. Lillie thought Josie never cared about how she would leave her home always, almost every night. Josie always left Lillie there and never said two words about it, but Lillie would never back talk her mother. Lillie was afraid of what was going to happen when she arrived at the hospital. The nurse saw all the blood and rushed Lillie into a room. Josie gave phony names because she wasn't going to pay no doctor bill. She then sat in the waiting room talking on the phone until the nurse called her into the room to hear the doctor's assessments. When Josie entered the room she saw Lillie laying in the bed and felt sorry for her. That is until the doctor told her Lillie had just gone through labor. Josie's eyes opened wide, her mouth dropped in shock. Josie was thinking . . . *Baby? I didn't even know she was pregnant. Then again she was always wearing big clothes.* Josie realized that she never took the time to notice of how Lillie looked and felt. That didn't matter anyway because now Josie was mad. She was mad at the fact she had a child and didn't tell her she was pregnant. Josie also wondered how it happened, who was the man? Josie glared angrily at Lillie. The stare scared Lillie; now she was afraid of what her mother was going to do to her.

Meanwhile a few doors over the baby girl was being looked at while Beulah and Curtis waited to hear the report. Later the doctor said they wanted to keep Lillie so Josie left the room to go smoke a cigarette. The nicotine from the cigarette relaxed Josie. Finally calming down, then Josie over heard two nurses talking. The women were talking about a baby that was left on top of a garbage can.

"Aint that a shame how someone left that baby outside on a garbage can!" one nurse said.

"Well whoever it is, is gonna be in big trouble when the police find out," the other nurse said. Josie threw her cigarette down and went back into the hospital to Lillie's room. "Get dressed! We gotta get out of here!" Josie yelled then helped Lillie get dressed and they slipped out passed everyone and drove off. As they were driving home Josie started up again with the yelling. Lillie sat there weak from all the pain and shaking with fear. "Why in the world would you leave a baby like that, what's wrong with you, and who you been screwing with, are you crazy? You want to end up like me? No life, surrounded by a bunch of brats!" Lillie began to cry, in her soft timid voice Lillie told her mother what had happened and who the man was. It was Lewis Parks a friend of her mother's. Josie drove the rest of the way home quiet. As mad as Josie wanted to be at Lillie, she knew it wasn't her fault. Josie felt shamed that one of her men friends came into her home and raped her daughter. When they got home Josie put her arm around Lillie and helped her into the house. Lillie was in so much pain, but she was happy to have her mother close to her. Josie laid Lillie in bed and put the covers over her. Lillie looked up at her mother with tears in her eyes. "Thank you mama, I love you." Josie turned away, turned off the lights and closed the door. She leaned back against the wall, her heart was heavy, and tears gently slid from her eyes. Josie knew what she was going to do to make this situation better. Josie made a phone call to her friend Blue, a big, black man who wanted her more than anything. Josie told Blue that she would take care of him if he took care of Lewis. Josie told Blue not to kill him but make him wish he was dead.

"How long we gonna stay up here Beulah?" Curtis asked. Beulah thought to herself: *There was a reason for the baby to be left at her house. Someone wanted her to care for that child; some woman that couldn't.* "Curtis, that baby is going to need a home, and if we can I want to keep her." Beulah told him.

"Honey, things are tight and the work is slow at the factory. How we gonna feed another mouth?" Curtis expressed. "God will make a way. He always does. We just got to keep the faith," Beulah said with a smile. They both waited a while longer then the doctor came out of the room and said the baby was not breathing regularly. The doctor let them know the baby would have to stay in the hospital a little longer. The doctor also told them the hospital and the police were working on locating the mother. "We had a possible suspect but she checked in under a phony name and left before we could question her. The child will go to the child protection service and be a ward of the state until we can find someone to adopt her," the doctor explained. Curtis and Beulah left, they made it clear they would be back to visit.

As days went by this baby girl fought for her life. Lying in an incubator the baby battled for survival. Beulah visited and prayed everyday. Curtis knew his wife wanted the child and he loved his wife so much he made several calls and had several conversations with a child protective service agent. Curtis discussed the steps necessary to adopt the baby. The agent told them they needed to complete some classes and go through a screening. Beulah was set on the idea and Curtis had to follow suit; each was willing to do what it took to make it happen. Weeks went by and the news talked of nothing but the headline story—the abandoned baby and her fate. Josie having snapped back into her normal evil self was scared someone would find out Lillie was the mother. If that were to happen Josie would lose her kids—which were her only source of income; baby Cindy was only two that meant a lot more time of free money. Josie told Lillie to keep her mouth shut; she was not to tell anyone about the baby and especially not Dorothy or Teresa. Josie didn't know that Lillie had no intentions of letting anyone know. She wanted her baby to have a life with love and happiness, not like the hell she was living in.

Later as time went on Beulah was at the hospital rocking the baby girl in her arms. She was now fully recovered and ready to leave. One of the nurses reminded Beulah the baby didn't have a name. Beulah smiled, looked down at the baby. The little baby looked up at Beulah with sparkling eyes. At that moment Beulah said, "I'm gonna name this baby Diamond. Just look at her eyes." Finally, after months of test, twenty-four hours surveillance, medication and shots, Diamond was ready to go home with her new family. Curtis and Beulah Bradford were both in their mid thirties. They lived in a small house with their two boys; Dennis—age twelve and Ricky—age ten. The couple moved in the small house three years before, Curtis was buying it. He worked as a laborer in a parts plant. Curtis was good at his job, he'd had worked there ten years and loved it. Beulah was a stay at home mom. She took care of the boys and the house while Curtis was at work. With things being slow at the plant finances were tight, but they were a Christian couple. They met at the Baptist church. They fell in love, got married and had their two beautiful children. And now they were adding an addition to their family. The boys were excited about having a little sister. All the family got together and prayed for the baby's future.

Time went on and things weren't looking good for the family. Curtis was working hard but the Bradfords were barely staying above water. Diamond was growing up healthy and now at three years old she was a busy and active little girl. She was a cute, tiny light skinned baby with curly hair and those big pretty sparkling eyes. The whole family loved that child. The boys were doing well in school and Beulah was happy with her family and home. The Bradford was struggling but they were happy, until Curtis came home with a look of defeat on his face. He told Beulah the plant had laid him off. The plant let one hundred men and women go and he was one of them. Curtis made parts for a bunch of major car companies, but business was slow so the company had to let Curtis and the others go. Curtis was upset because he had a family to take care of. The plant was discussing a yearlong layoff period. Curtis couldn't wait that long. Beulah told Curtis she would have to look for work; but they needed someone to keep Diamond, but the cost of day care was too high. Curtis thought to himself: *I knew something like this would happen. I don't know what to make of this. I don't want my wife to work, and even if I wanted her to she can't now because of the baby. I love Diamond but at the same time this is someone else's child that I'm feeding and clothing. While who knows where her parents are.*

Lillie was eighteen years old now. She never went to school and was still at home taking care of her mother and her mother's kids. Danny was twelve, Keith was eleven and Cindy was five and a handful. Cindy thought of Lillie as her mother because Josie was usually gone or sleeping in her room with the door shut while Lillie took full responsibility for the running of the household. Billy her brother when he was old enough to see how bad Josie treated Lillie was upset. Billy couldn't stand to see his mother yelling at Lillie. One day as Josie was yelling at Lillie, Lillie stood there not saying anything with big sad eyes. Josie was screaming over something so small. She was yelling because Lillie forgot to tell her about a man who called. Billy was tired of seeing his sister being broken down. Billy stepped up to defend Lillie; he and his mother had a big blow out. He said, "If you would stay home sometimes and do something other than sleep, you could get your own phone calls!" "I know you ain't up in my house talking to me this way boy. Do you know I will take the time to personally whoop yo ass!" Josie yelled back "Mama you know you ain't gonna whoop me. That would mean you would have to give me some attention, and you know you don't have time for any of us, and that's okay with me. But Lillie wants your love. Whenever she talks it's about how not to make noise or mess the house up so mama won't be mad or how she cooks things she thinks you will like and you walk past without saying anything!" Billy said upset.

"Look boy, if you don't like it here why don't you follow your sister Rainy and get out!" Josie screamed. That was enough for Billy. Billy packed up his things to stay with his grandmother and sister Rainy. Before he left he tried to get Lillie to go with him. Lillie just said in her soft voice, "I'll never leave Mama, she needs me." Billy just shook his head and left. Lillie didn't want to see Billy leave but deep down inside she was glad he would be somewhere where he could be happy. Lillie knew their home was not a happy place it was just a house, not a home. She knew all the kids would leave someday, but not her. She couldn't leave her mother because she loved her and she would take the abuse because she knew her mother was unhappy and needed love. With that thought Lillie thought about her own baby girl. Lillie was glad the baby never had to enter Josie's house. This was her life and her problem to bear. She wanted her daughter to have a life, go to school, have friends, and have a family of her own one day with a husband and children.

After six months had gone by Curtis and Beulah couldn't pay

the mortgage and lost their home. They all moved into a three bedroom Duplex. Curtis was still laid off and unemployment was not enough to cover all of the bills, he was hurt. He felt like he had let his family down. Beulah said one day, "We'll get another house, and if we don't so what? As long as we have each other and we are all healthy we will make it. Honey you just got to have faith and believe God will make away. We loss a house but think Curtis, it's only a house, what if it were a child?" Curtis had to agree with his wife; it could have been worst, but still he felt he had failed. The duplex was smaller than their old house, and they didn't have very good neighbors either. There were gangs all through the neighborhood, everyone was poor, houses were getting broken into and there was always a fight outside. Two months later the plant called Curtis back to work. Both Curtis and Beulah decided they wouldn't move until they were sure about Curtis' job and how long he'd be working before the next lay off. They decided to wait but as soon as they could get their kids out of the area they would.

Diamond was now five years old, her two brothers Ricky and Dennis were both in high school. Curtis and Beulah had the family in church to try to keep them away from the gangs. They knew the kids would choose something to occupy their time they just prayed it would be the Lord. One Sunday as the whole family went to church and five-year-old Diamond was singing in the kid's choir. Diamond was so beautiful up their clapping and singing with the rest of the children. Beulah was misty-eyed watching her and taking pictures when Beulah saw another little girl that looked a lot like Diamond. A few benches over Missionary Dorothy sat with all her grand children. Dorothy was trying to make a point taking all of them to church, especially Lillie. Lillie needed to get out of the house and try to have a life. She was twenty years old now and she never had a boyfriend and she didn't want one after being raped and Lillie knew her mother would not allow her to have one. When Dorothy called and told Josie she was coming to get the rest of her grandchildren and take them to church Josie couldn't argue with that. Lillie loved church, the feeling she got when she was there made her feel good. She was happy to see her sister Cindy up there singing with the kid's choir. Then Lillie's eyes shifted to another little girl, she was cute and she looked familiar. When they did the next selection Diamond led the song. The whole church lit up. Curtis and Beulah were so proud when the children were finished singing they were lead to the back of the church for their own children's service. The pastor got up and said "I enjoyed the babies singing and how that little girl Diamond was going places. To think five years ago somebody tried to throw her away. She was left on top of a trashcan but Brother and Sister Bradford took this Diamond in the rough into their home and into their lives. Look how good God is." The children walked down the side hall where they could be seen yet they could not hear the pastor speaking.

Wow! Lillie thought, that's my baby, she is so beautiful and lively. How could that be my child? Lillie wanted to go hug her baby. Those people didn't understand she didn't try to throw away her baby. She was scared and didn't know what to do. She was trying to take her baby somewhere safe. Lillie remembered the face of the couple; she never forgot it and she thought about them and the baby everyday. She wondered how her daughter was doing; she went back to their house and saw they had moved that tore her up. But now here she was in a good family, going to church and the smile on her face let Lillie know she did the right thing. Tears started to flow from her eyes as she watched her daughter disappear down the hall with the rest of the children. When Dorothy saw how emotional Lillie was she thought she was just in the spirit. Dorothy was glad to see anything other than sad, gloomy, timid looks Lillie usually had.

Through out the service Lillie thought about her child, wondering what would happen if she told everyone, that Diamond was her daughter. Would Diamond be happy to see her real mother? But then Lillie knew it would disrupt the child's life and confuse her. Dorothy would be upset because no one told her and Dorothy would definitely be mad at Josie. Those nice people might get upset and most importantly Josie would be mad. Lillie couldn't have that, so she stayed quiet. When the church service was over and everyone was leaving, Lillie and her brothers and sisters were waiting at the church door while their Grandmother was talking to some of the members that were leaving. Curtis and Beulah and the children approached her. Dorothy stopped them to talk and Lillie watched how Diamond stayed next to her new mother holding her hand. Dorothy leaned down and told Diamond how she loved her singing and then the two ladies talked about the service, while both families stood around waiting. Lillie was shaking and breaking out in sweat. She was so nervous and emotional standing next to her baby who was looking up at Lillie and smiling at her. She was smiling like she knew. Tears started flowing again from Lillie. She was about ready to burst, when finally Curtis told Beulah it was time to go. Lillie watched sadly as her baby daughter, walked off in got into their car and drove off. Lillie was glad about one thing she would see more of Diamond in church and later at school; where Diamond was going with Cindy who was her aunt.

CHAPTER 4

Badtimes All Around

Hard times hit again and after five years had gone by, Curtis was laid off again. They had moved into a nicer home so it was really hard to make ends meet. Dennis was off to college that Curtis was trying to pay for. Diamond was in school and spending time at home learning how to cook and clean. Beulah was also teaching her how to be a nice young lady. The children were getting along fine, all except Ricky. No matter how they tried Curtis and Beulah could not keep him from joining a gang. It was hard for Diamond watching as Curtis and Ricky argued every time he came home. Ricky trying to be hard so he would curse and get into gang fights to fit in. Curtis threatened to throw him out, but Curtis didn't have the heart to. One day Curtis found a gun in Ricky's room, Curtis was at the end of his rope with Ricky. They got into a huge fistfight Beulah was crying, Dennis, who was home from college tried to stop the fight, and little Diamond hugged her mother tight because she was scared and confused, she wondered what happened to their happy home. After Dennis got them apart Curtis yelled, "Boy I brought you here, I'll take you out next time you put your hands on me!" "Pops I'm a grown ass man you can't be whooping me. I'm from the hard core, I don't fist fight anymore, and somebody else would have been shot for less than you did!" Ricky yelled back. "Oh you bad walking around with yo gun. You thinking you can't be hurt. You ain't the only one with a gun, and if you live by the sword, you'll die by the sword. You better remember that. And if you are so grown, why are you living here!" "I don't need to stay here; I got plenty of places to lay my head!" Ricky screamed. And with that Ricky walked across the room gave both his mother and sister a kiss and left. A week later Curtis and Beulah were called to the hospital to identify his body. Ricky had been shot during a gang war.

The family went through this storm with everyone blaming their self, for Ricky's death. Every one of them thinking, if they could have said something or did something different. Ricky would still be alive. People kept coming over trying to comfort the family by telling them it was his time to go. The people would tell them that it was in God's plan, like Ricky didn't have anything to do with it. "Why do people do harmful things to them selves and expect God to keep coming through for them. It's like putting your hand in a flame and praying you don't get burned. After a while people are going to have to realize you can't expect God to keep taking care of the stupid things we do. We have to be accountable for ourselves. God gives each one of us the tools necessary to avoid dangerous situations. If we try to live a good, saved life I do believe he will protect us from harm. Unless HE says it's our time to go. Now that's planned, not what happened to our son." Curtis said with tears in his eyes. The family tried to pull it together as much as they could but it was a very hard time for them.

The day of the funeral some of the church members stopped by their home to pay their respects. Dorothy said she was going to take Cindy to be with Diamond, they had become very good friends in school. Because they were so close and looked so much a like the other kids called them sisters. Dorothy thought Cindy would want to comfort her friend, but Dorothy was surprised when Lillie wanted to go too. Dorothy was happy Lillie wanted to get out of the house. Lillie never went anywhere other than church and the grocery store. That was starting to bother Dorothy. Lillie was twenty-five years old and she didn't have any goals dreams or friends, not even a boyfriend. She was always too scared and shy to talk, but now she was asking to tag along with Dorothy. That was a big step for Lillie. Lillie and Dorothy took some cakes they had baked to the Bradford's home. Lillie stood close to her grandmother while she talked with Beulah. After a few minutes Lillie managed to pull herself away and found Diamond and Cindy who was playing in Diamond's bedroom in the back and talking about school. Lillie stood in the doorway watching them and admiring how each of the girls had grown. Cindy noticed her sister standing at the door told her to come in the room. Then Cindy introduced Lillie to Diamond who said hello and smiled. Lillie just stood there looking at her. Lillie so desperately wanted to grab Diamond and hug her and kiss her and tell her she loved her. She wanted to tell Diamond she was her mother and she didn't abandon her, she just wanted her to have a good life and be happy. Lillie's heart was racing but she knew this was not the time to confess. Lillie sat down and watched as Cindy and Diamond talked about young girl stuff. Lillie noticed Diamond had a cute little room. Her own room, more than she would have back at her mama house. Hours went by, Dorothy was ready to leave, Lillie didn't want to go but it was getting late. When Cindy and Lillie got up to leave Diamond thanked them for coming over and hugged both Cindy and Lillie. Lillie was so overwhelmed she hugged Diamond tight and didn't want to let go. She didn't want to leave Diamond but she knew she could see her another time. On the drive home Dorothy noticed Lillie had a big smile on her face. This was shocking, and then Dorothy started to realize how Lillie always acted different around the Bradford family. When Lillie and Cindy got home Josie was waiting on them. When the girls walked in the house Josie slapped Lillie hard across the face, because all of the kids except Lillie and Cindy were gone. Danny and Keith had moved in with Dorothy and Josie was upset, she hated when the house was empty. Cindy ran to her room while Josie yelled at Lillie for not being home. Lillie stood there and listened until Josie left the house. Lillie wasn't going to let anyone even Josie steal her joy. She went to her room and thanked God for letting her be able to be around her child.

After everyone had left Curtis told Beulah he couldn't take the neighborhood anymore. He didn't want anything happening to Dennis or Diamond, so a few months later they packed up and moved to a nicer area.

Curtis wanted a change; they moved into a small house on the other side of town. Changed churches and Diamond transferred schools. The school was different it had more rich kids. Diamonds family was still struggling so she didn't have all of the nice expensive clothes everyone else had. She had old clothes but they were always clean and neat. But kids were cruel and teased her all through grade school. Diamond didn't care too much about that, she was into learning. Even as a young child Curtis and Beulah noticed how Diamond was always trying to invent better ways to do things. Diamond grew beautiful, nicely shaped, light skinned, long flowing hair and an eye for designer clothes. She couldn't afford them so she would draw outfits and designs every time she got the chance.

Time past and Diamond started high school and Curtis was still working at the plant. Beulah was still taking care of the home. Dennis had graduated from college and had a good job. He was also married and expecting his second child Curtis and Beulah were excited and proud of their son. Then Diamond entered high school with high hopes. She was very smart and loved to create and invent new things. She had so many ideals and like grade school—she was teased because of her clothes. They were simple nothing extravagant or 'top of the line' like the other girls. The kids were mean to her, and they made fun of her constantly. Curtis didn't have a lot of money to spend on clothes he spent most of the money he made on the rent. Diamond understood she would tell her parents that one day she would buy them their own house. But until then Diamond's only friends were poor kids like her self. Diamond's best friend was Felisha Daniels. They met freshmen year. Felisha was a quiet, small figured, brown skinned girl. She always wore braids in her hair and it always took a long time before she got them redone. She couldn't afford to get them redone as often as she needed to so she would normally walk around with fuzzy braids until she had the money to get a fresh set. None of that mattered to Diamond. Felisha was Diamond's home girl, they would go to the mall and look at outfits and tell each other what they would buy if they had the money. Felisha loved clothes and like Diamond she would draw sketches of outfits and share them with Diamond. They would talk for hours and hours on the phone. Diamond and Felisha respected each other; and everything was cool between them until Ted Banks enter their lives. Ted was a senior; he was a tall built, basketball star and he tried to talk to both of them. The girls recognized what was going on and unlike a lot of other girls they wouldn't and didn't let him break up their friendship. Felisha would say men come and go but sometimes you only get one true friend. Diamond felt that Felisha was more than a friend she was more of a sister. When it came time to graduate Diamond's heart broke when she found out Felisha was moving to California to live with her father. Diamond was so sad when Felisha left. Diamond told Curtis and Beulah she was glad they didn't split up and have her and Dennis moving back and forth between them. Beulah looked at Curtis sadly and that night while lying in bed they decide they would tell Diamond she was adopted. They kept it from her waiting to tell her when she was old enough, then they decided to wait until they had to, this was that time.

The next morning while Beulah and Curtis sat at the breakfast table Diamond walked in the kitchen still sad that Felisha had moved. She slumped down in the chair to eat breakfast. That's when Beulah started to talk. "Diamond, you know we all love you. Curtis Dennis, and Ricky when he was alive, God rest his soul and myself. That will never change, but its time we tell you something that we hope won't change the way you feel about us." Diamond was now getting really nervous listening to her mother and trying to understand what she was getting at. Curtis and Beulah were sitting there looking so serious. "This isn't good, she thought. But it can't be worst than Felisha moving away" she thought-WRONG. Beulah started to continue then she broke down and started crying. Diamond started to tear up just watching her mother; even Curtis was being affected by the tears. Curtis knew he had to let Diamond know the truth. "Baby were not your birth parents, we adopted you when you were a baby, when someone left you in our backyard." "What!" Diamond was shocked to no means. She just looked at this couple; these people she called her mother and father, the only parents she knew. Tears racing down Diamond's face she struggled to say, "I don't understand why you didn't tell me before. And who is my real mother and father?" "We don't know Diamond all we know is that you were just born and someone left you on top of our garbage can in left. We didn't feel ready to tell you that until we figured you could handle it," Curtis said. "And you think I can handle it now Daddy?! I can't, I wish you wouldn't have ever told me. Now I feel like trash, that's why I was being thrown away!" Diamond said crying uncontrollably. Beulah then told her, "Whoever it was, was probably leaving you to us, because they knew we would love and care for you more than they could." Both Curtis and Beulah held on to Diamond while she cried. She then went upstairs to her room and vowed she would do well in life. She would show everyone how she could go from a garbage can to a mansion. Diamond laid in her bed; as her mind drifted into a sleepy haze she wondered about her birth mother.

CHAPTER 5

From Garbage Can to Mansion

Lillie now in her thirties was still living at home. Cindy was in her early twenties and already had three kids. She moved out and was going down the same path as Josie. Cindy's children had no father's in their lives and she had no skills. Lillie had to go out and get a job to pay bills since Josie was no longer receiving any welfare checks. Lillie found a job at the Hunters parts plant where Curtis worked at. Lillie had worked there a few weeks and liked the ideal of getting out of the house and having a Job. Even though Josie would take her whole check—leaving her with only a few dollars. Lillie didn't care; after the Bradfords had moved away Lillie was heartsick. Not being able to see her child was depressing. Lillie moped and was much sadder than usual. When Cindy left it was only Lillie and Josie remaining. Lillie was lonely because Josie was gone most of the time and like before, if she was present she was sleeping. So it was lonely going from a house full of kids to the emptiness and not knowing where Diamond was, so she could at least see how she was growing up, this tore her up. Lillie wondered where she was, what she doing, and she even wondered if Diamond wanted to know who she was. Lillie wanted to see her and how she had grown up. So when she saw Curtis at the plant Lillie was so happy, she couldn't wait till the end of the day to talk to him. It had to have been a miracle. Lillie saw Curtis getting into his car so Lillie called to him in her soft voice; he didn't hear her so she had to call again. Curtis turned around to see Lillie standing there looking at him. Curtis wondered what this lady wanted—he didn't recognize her at first. Lillie was just standing there scared to open her mouth, until Curtis remembered her and how she used to do that at the old church. "I know you, you're Dorothy's granddaughter. I was sorry to hear she passed years ago." Curtis said. Lillie thought about how that was a sad time for them and how hard Josie took it. [Josie was also torn up about the fact that she left every thing to Teresa and all of the grand kids]. Dorothy wrote a letter saying that she couldn't leave her hard earned money she and her husband worked for to someone who would drink and gamble it all up. Dorothy also said in the letter that she was sorry she couldn't leave Lillie anything because she knew Josie would get it. But she wanted to let Lillie know that she loved her with all her heart. Lillie didn't care about money she knew Dorothy loved her and Lillie loved her back. When Dorothy died that was yet another broken piece of Lillie's heart. This man that was standing in front of Lillie, he was the very person that could help repair Lillie's broken heart. "How's the family?" Lillie asked softly. "Everyone is fine, Dennis is married and having kids, Beulah is doing well and Diamond," when Curtis said her name Lillie eyes lit up. Curtis stepped back for a moment. Lillie's eyes lit up just the way Diamond's did. He then went on to finish his statement. "Diamond finished high school and was about to start college." Lillie said thank you, and that it was nice to see him and how glad she was to hear his family was doing well. Lillie turned toward the street and made her way to the bus stop she got on the bus smiling to her self. She was happy to hear that her daughter was doing well.

Diamond enrolled in the local college in town; her major was business. She already was smart and watched a lot of business channels on TV. She even read books on how to run a successful business. To most of the freshmen students the classes were hard to Diamond they were simple and she took all the classes the school had to offer. She did so well she graduated top of the class a year early and had several job offers. Diamond was so focused throughout college that she stayed in the books. She went on very few dates—[most of the men she went on dates couldn't handle such a driven woman]. Diamond got jobs through college to pay for the things she could not afford growing up; things like clothes, shoes and accessories. She bought her clothes cheap but the way she put them together gave the clothes a unique flair. A lot of the other ladies on campus thought she spent big money on her stylish arrangements—but she never did. Curtis was helping her as much as he could and Diamond was grateful for that, she would never take advantage of him by buying expensive clothes with money that could go toward purchasing her books. Diamond told herself that one-day she was going to get her daddy out of that dead end plant job that worked him so hard. Curtis would come home, shower sit in his chair and fall right to sleep. Sometimes he would fall asleep before he even ate dinner. That hurt both Beulah and Diamond's to see that, but Curtis was glad to help his daughter as he did for Dennis. Curtis wished he could have done the same for Ricky but he was gone.

Now at twenty-three years old Diamond was ready for the world. She looked over her job offers and decided to start at the top. Diamond accepted a position at the top investment firm in the area, Smith and Smith investment Corp. Diamond had several recommendations from people within the company and her teachers. Turner Smith a thirty year old, dark hair white man— the son of Tim Smith—owner and CEO was told Diamond had a good head on her shoulders. She was dedicated, motivated, and innovative and knew her stuff when it came down to dollars and cents. Tim didn't want to hire Diamond; he already had on black woman on the payroll—Teresa Morgan. Teresa was all the color he needed in his company. Actually having her was almost too much and he only kept her to handle black clients. Turner talked Tim into giving Diamond a try. Turner told his father that if she was as good as people said she was, they wouldn't want her working for the competition. Diamond was overjoyed when she walked into her small furnish office. It smelled like citrus wood polish and success. Diamond was on her way. She moved out of her parent's home into a small apartment near the office. She also bought a cute little used car. DIAMOND WAS READY FOR THE WORLD. Diamond thought she could tackle the universe. Anything anyone dished out she could take it and serve it right back to them. Diamonds head was inflated three times its normal size, but when she showed up on her first day she got a real dose of corporate America. The company was made up entirely of middle age white men—stuffy white men. The only comfort she found aside from her office was seeing the only sister in the building looking like she was running things. Diamond thought to herself, I want to be just like her.

Teresa was in her early fifties. She was elegant; she wore a stylish short haircut that accented her strong jaw line. She wore a nave blue skirt suit that looked like it cost a pretty penny. Teresa was glad to see another sister in the business. When Teresa went over to Diamond to introduce herself she was shocked to see how much this young girl looked like her niece Lillie; it was blowing her mind. After they got acquainted the whole group of associates sat down to go over some business. Diamond looked and listened with her undivided attention. She was taking it all in, all the information she needed. Diamond knew she was at the bottom of the totem pole but she was going to work her way to the top. Teresa could see how hungry for success Diamond was. Teresa admired Diamond's passion, she decided she would take Diamond under her wing, Teresa would become her mentor. It didn't take long for Teresa and Diamond to become close. Diamond made Teresa wish she had taken time out of her life to have a daughter like her. Teresa wanted to be a successful businesswoman. After watching her Sister Josie having so many children and doing nothing else. Teresa couldn't see herself living the same way. She loved her nieces and nephews but her life was dedicated to business. That's what Teresa took to bed at night—thoughts of deals, investments, joint ventures and contract terms. Teresa wasn't going to date any man that wasn't up to her standards. He had to be making the same amount or more money than she was making and unfortunately all the men in this category were either married or with a white woman. Teresa was not going to settle. So she spent a lot of lonely nights. She didn't have many friends because she was a workaholic. Her mother was gone now and her sister was a waste of sperm she thought. So having Diamond around was a good thing. Teresa was teaching Diamond everything she knew about the investment business and Diamond took it all in. She was learning more and more everyday with Teresa helping her. Diamond was thrilled to have Teresa in her life at that time because Diamond was always away from home and didn't know anyone. After a few months Teresa and Diamond were really close. Teresa had to catch herself from sometimes talking to Diamond as a daughter instead of a colleague.

At the office the Smiths would have Diamond doing easy

secretary jobs, fetching coffee and doing mail runs. Diamond was getting fed-up, but one of the associates named Marshal Burns— an older, slim, gray harried white man with thick glasses was very respectful to Diamond. He even gave her a few tips about the business. He told her how to get clients, help them to invest and produce their ideals. He thought Diamond was a real go getter and if the company lost her she would be a force to be reckoned with. Marshal could see Diamond had that drive in her eyes. He would tell her to hold on and not get upset; he knew the Smiths were giving her a hard time because she should have had the chance to work with the clients by now. Marshal knew they had done Teresa the same way; he could see if she held out a little longer she would be just as successful as Teresa. It was a long while before Teresa was able to see clients. She only had a few and they were mostly black. Teresa worked hard for clients and made a lot of money for the company. She was hoping if she did a good job with the few clients she got the Smiths would recognize her talent and trust her with more clients. After watching Diamond go through the same struggle she had gone through years ago, she knew neither one of them would get the same respect as the white associates. There were no steps leading up, no matter how hard Teresa worked for her clients or how much money she made for the company she would never be elevated from the position she currently held. Teresa blew up one day, she told the Smiths to stick her job where the sun don't shine and quit. Diamond was hurt to see Teresa leave but Diamond was just starting and she knew what it took to get to the top. Her first plan of action was presenting some of her ideals.

One day she asked to speak with Mr. Smith Sr. When she entered the room she was ready, she sat down with him and Marshal and laid her notes on the table. Diamond talked about how she wanted to go further in the company. She wanted to help the company expand and grow; she believed through her ideas she could help the company reach new heights and increase its revenue. Mr. Smith looked and listened. He had a big smile pasted on his face, that smile gave Diamond the impression the meeting went well. After Diamond left Mr. Smith took the notes she left for him to view and said "When the day comes where we need a

Nigger to take our company higher, it won't be a company." Mr. Smith then threw her notes in the trash tin next to the conference table. With that Mr. Smith exited the room-leaving Marshal sitting there disgusted. Marshal couldn't believe the fact that Mr. Smith was still living in the sixties with his racist attitude. Marshal rescued Diamonds ideas from the trash and left the room. When he got back to his office he spread the pages across his desk and began to read. He started writing and calculating. When Marshal finished going over the notes he laughed out loud. A few minutes later Marshal called Diamond in his office.

"Diamond I'm not going to bull shit you Mr. Smith was just humoring you. He doesn't respect you as an employee or even a person for that matter. He's a racist pig and before you got here I decided to submit my resignation. The only notice he's gonna get is today when I walk out that door were gonna wipe his company off the map! After getting your notes out of the trash I looked at your ideas. Your methods of getting, keeping and satisfying clients are excellent. I'll invest the start up money because I believe you can make this happen." Diamond sat there taking it all in. She was hurt someone would think her ideas were garbage and now because of hater's like that she was going to show them her life was not trash. Diamond told Marshal she would do it as long as she had complete control—she knew what she wanted and how. Marshal assured her, "This is your baby. I'm only buying the carriage to get it rolling." They shook hands Diamond was so excited she hugged Marshal and left. Minutes later Diamond charged down the hallway to Mr. Smith's office. Diamond snatched his glass doors open and walked right passed his secretary. The small blonde woman called after Diamond in her squeaky voice, "Excuse me ma'am, um excuse me, you don't have an appointment, you-." Diamond never stopped to look at the woman she called over shoulder, and said "This won't take long." Diamond walked right into Mr. Smith's personal office and walked over to his desk grabbed a scrap of paper and wrote on it. In big black letters I QUIT! She showed him the paper and tossed it in the trash, the same way he had done her ideas. "You see where I threw that paper? That's where your company's gonna be when I get through with you!" Diamond said then walked out of there confidant. She looked the secretary up and down and said, "See I told you it wouldn't take long." Diamond let herself out of the last set of doors, and down the hall to her small office to collect her things. Diamond loaded her few items into her car and called Teresa on her way home.

Diamond filled Teresa in on the play out of the whole day adding dramatic suspense. Teresa nearly choked laughing at Diamond and the whole situation. When Diamond finish telling Teresa how she told the Smiths off she got right down to business. Teresa listened with her undivided attention. She was excited and couldn't wait to start. Diamond Marshal and Teresa were ready to start a new adventure for all of them. Marshal bought a small building and a few pieces of furniture; it was simple but neat. That didn't matter though, because as soon as the doors were open clients came pouring in. THE DIAMOND CORPORATION was now in BUSINESS. Diamond was CEO, Marshal was President and Teresa was appointed Vice President. To level the playing field Diamond decided that she was going to do exactly what Smith and Smith didn't do. Diamond and her board were going to break through the color barrier and give professional minorities an opportunity to showcase their corporate abilities.

They hired Rita Jasper, a young, thin, plain looking, white woman. Rita was intelligent and had an excellent business sense; she was always passed over at her last job, and because she was not a looker she always got the shaft. Cory Carrington, a young black man fresh out of college—[Diamond thought she would give him a better chance than she had when she got out of school]. Juan Lopez, a middle aged Hispanic man. He was smart, well spoken and passionate about his work. He would have been an asset to any company but was looked over because of his ethnicity. Juan had to take a labor job to feed his family, when he was offered the opportunity to do what he loved he jumped on it. Last was Derrick West, a middle age, handsome black man Teresa met at a business seminar. Derrick heard how a group of people was starting a new company and he decided to look into it. When Derrick saw Teresa, he convinced her to give him a try. Diamond respected Teresa so much that she gave Derrick a job but the warning signs were up. With both the old and new associates the Diamond Corporation definitely had an awesome team. Diamond got them all together and explained what she wanted and how she wanted it done Their Company was going to be different. They weren't going to overcharge for their services and they weren't going to trick their clients into investing into businesses that didn't suit them or make money. The Diamond Corporation was going to run a business of quality and integrity. Derrick had a problem with the fee he felt by charging so little the company would never make money. Diamond leaned back in her chair and looked at everyone. "My company is going to be built on trust and loyalty with our client's best interest in mind. And you will find that a happy client is a good business. Happy clients are free advertisement and free recruiters that in turn create revenue." That aspect had never dawned on Derrick. Marshal beaming from his seat next to Diamond, He was proud to be a part of her Team. With Smith and Smith Marshal he had some money, but after all of those years of service all he had was a couple hundred thousand dollars. Money he was glad to give to finance the start of this company that was soon to creep its way to the top of the corporate world. Marshal had faith Diamond would take the company far. After the meeting, Derrick noticed how close Teresa and the boss were. Derrick knew what he had to do to stay in good with the big boss lady. He walked over to the two ladies and started laying it on thick. He went on and on about how proud he was of both Teresa and Diamond. He rambled on about how two beautiful black sisters—or sistahs as he called them were doing big business. Diamond was not falling for his butt kissing, but Teresa was lost in his bull crap. Diamond noticed how Teresa was looking like a schoolgirl falling for the lame conversation he was throwing at them. After everyone left Diamond and Marshal stayed behind to go over the meeting. "What do you think about our team?" Marshal asked. "Marshal I think we have a great group of hungry people. I believe each one of them is ready to put Diamond Corp. on the map. Let's talk about our first line of attack, but please excuse me if I don't sit down. My ass hurts from all that kissing up Derrick did earlier" Diamond and Marshal both laughed.

Rita was a go-getter; she got the company's name out there and won major business for Dcorp. Rita pitched the Dcorp so well companies from all over were testing the water. After each company got a glimpse of what Diamond and her team was capable of they climbed aboard. The businesses saw that Dcorp was different; they were not overcharging or forcing the businesses into foolish investment. Those investing knew Dcorp was looking out for the interest for their businesses and finances. Before long Dcorp had so many clients they had to hire more associates. Diamond then picked Rita, Juan, Cory and Derrick to be on the executive board along with Marshal, Teresa and herself. Several of Teresa and Marshal's clients at Smith and Smith made the switch to Dcorp. With the initial switch of a few of Smith and Smith clients the word spread and huge chunk of their clients then crossed over to Diamond's company. This left Smith and Smith only a faithful few. The name of the game was money making and many of the investors saw they could make more money and it would cost them less to do so. Who wouldn't seize that opportunity? Diamond showed you can charge a few people a lot of money, but by cutting cost and catering to a larger scale of people you can make more money, and they did. The money was rolling in.

The first order of business was to pay back all the money Marshal spent to get it started. Marshal was overwhelmed; he didn't realize how quickly the company would take off. He was just glad to be involved; he knew Dcorp was the start of something big. The whole team was making money. Marshal had doubled his investment in six months. Rita and Juan spent money on their families, Cory put the majority of his money in the bank, and Derrick bought a home a couple of cars and loads of expensive clothes. Teresa was already well off and just had more money to put away that appealed to Derrick. Diamond remembered the day she told Curtis and Beulah about the company. She thought back to that evening when they got on their knees and prayed for the success of the business. None of them could believe the company blew up almost over night. They had so many clients several of their competitors had to close, including Smith and Smith. Diamond, Teresa and Marshal went out together and celebrated when they heard the news. Later Diamond felt bad, she knew she was taught better than that. No matter how bad the Smiths had treated her she felt it was wrong to rejoice in their failure.

As Diamond drove up to her parent's small home, her mind went back to the time she spent there. She reminisced over the time when they all had to buckle up and pinch pennies. Her mind went back to the times where Curtis struggled to put food on the table. The times he worked till he had nothing left but somehow Curtis always made ends meet. He did all that he could for his family even though Diamond was someone else's child it seemed like he worked the hardest for her. He would work long back, breaking hours and overtime on top of that just to put Diamond through school. Without him and Beulah supporting her, Diamond knew she would not had made it, and for that she felt she needed to repay them. When she came into the house both of them were sitting in their chairs in the living room watching TV. "Hey big company girl," Curtis smiled. Both he and Beulah were proud of Diamond and happy for her success. Diamond sat down with them and turned the TV off. She put on a serious face. "I have something to tell you. If it weren't for you two loving me and taking care of me, who knows where I would be. Now I have a company that is growing and expanding everyday but what good is wealth if you can't take care of the ones you love. So, mom, dad I have the privilege of doing some thing for you guys."

A couple of weeks later Diamond bought her parent's a brand new house and a brand new truck for Curtis. Curtis had tears in his eyes remembering back to the times when he struggled to feed her, now she was buying them a home and a truck. Beulah was ecstatic, she was going from room to room thinking about how she was going to decorate. Diamond had given her a big check to buy furniture. As Christians each of them knew exactly who to give the glory to.

In a few short years of service Diamond Corp. had turned into a fortune500 company, with international clients to add to all of the rest. Diamond Bradford was a multi- millionairist and the money kept pouring in. Every endeavor Diamond dove into seem to blow up and make nothing but profit. She was now in the position to put her clothing designs to work. After Diamond opened Diamond Corp. Diamond hired a seamstress to sew clothes she had designed herself. Everywhere she went she was complimented on her wardrobe. Teresa was convinced she should submit her designs to a clothing store, she did. Once she submitted her designs she was confident she could start her own clothing line. Diamond bought her own building and called it Diamond Fashion. Diamond Fashion was getting so many orders Marshal set up more stores outside the area. Life was great Diamond bought the mansion she had always dreamed of. It was huge, it had twenty bedrooms, ten bathrooms, and sunken living room all decked out in white fur. She had a marble dining table that sat twenty; on the other side of the mansion there was a theater room that sat fifty. The mansion had a deluxe great room that was made into her personal rec.-room. It had a big screen TV, pool table, card table, an area couch that circled around the TV, a full bar and glass doors that opened to the backyard. In the backyard there was an elevated covered porch area with lounge chairs that overlooked the swimming pool and Jacuzzi. Yards away there was a tennis court. In the garage Diamond had a gold Cadillac with the license that read Diamond#1.The red Corvette was Diamond#2, Diamond#3 was the black on black Range Rover and last but not least was Diamond#4—a pearl white limo. Diamond also had a four bedroom guesthouse where she normally stayed. There was also another cute home on Diamond's property where her house keeping staff stayed. They were a Hispanic family, the father Jose was the ground keeper, and the mother Maria did all of the cooking and cleaning and their two teenagers Maurie and Edmond would help out when they were not busy with schoolwork. The family worked well, was paid well and stayed in their home rent-free. Diamond was all about being better than fair. As Diamond walked through her house one day she looked around and said, "I made it!" but she thought, but *why does it feel like something*

is missing?

CHAPTER 6

Who's the Boss?

Diamond knew exactly what was missing in her life. Sadly, most of the men that came into her life were rich, spoiled and didn't have a clue on having a good time. They only wanted to boast, brag or discuss business. Unfortunately Diamond was surrounded by those types of men, she put her love life on hold to make a name for herself and that she did. Diamond Corporation now was known in all of the fifty states and in many countries. The world was exposed to Dcorp. But very few people knew Diamond personal, she made it a goal to keep her face behind the scenes, she found that it worked better that way. When people started to notice Dcorp as a growing company the fake and the phonies started to pour in; Diamond realize the more money you have the more 'so called friends' you have.

Diamond was sitting at her desk in her newly remodeled office and decided to call her mother. She was shocked to hear her father's voice on the other end of the telephone. "What are you doing home daddy?" she asked. "I'm home because they had another lay off Di. I've been there for over thirty years and still they laid me off. I know it because I'm old. I don't know what them big heads up there in them offices are doing, but a lot of the workers are gonna go hungry." Diamond knew her father wasn't going to have to worry about income but Curtis' pride was strong. That was the very reason he didn't want his wife to work and he wasn't going to let his daughter support him. Curtis was a man. Diamond had bought them a beautiful home and the nicest truck on the lot he wasn't excepting anything else. After hanging up the phone Diamond thought, *How many times were these people having lay offs and why? My daddy has been at this plant for years and he's been laid off just about ever four years, and sometimes the lay off would last close to a year. I know we struggled, and if we struggled I know some of the other workers had it worse than us.*

Lillie was laid off along with a lot of the others. Curtis showed her how to apply for unemployment. It wasn't what she was getting at her job so it was barely enough to pay the rent, utilities, and food. The pay cut meant Josie couldn't go out and party as much as she liked. Being that Josie was older now late fifties she didnt get as many men calling on her as they used to. Most of the men she brought home would try to get next to Lillie, which made Josie jealous. At forty-two Lillie was finally coming out of her shell now that she had started working and interacting with people. Yet and still Lillie was quiet and only spoke when she was spoken to. Before Lillie wouldn't speak at all unless there was a dire situation and because Lillie was so quiet Curtis was the only one to befriend her at the plant. Sometimes he would sit and have lunch with her Curtis would often wonder what happened to her to make her so timid and scared.

"Look Lillie I think you better find another job to bring some more money into this house! I took care of you all your life, and kept you out of jail by not telling the cops about that baby you threw away!" Josie yelled. Lillie sat on the couch with her head down near tears as her mother screamed at her. Josie was in one of her moods and now she was on a roll, once she started screaming she couldn't be stopped until she was satisfied and had hurt Lillie's feelings. Josie hollered about the usual, how Lillie ruined her life, how she could have made something of herself if Lillie was not born. When Josie screamed it was somewhat routine, but at the same time it always hurt Lillie. Josie was running out of things to yell about so Lillie was preparing to get up wipe her face and go about her business. Lillie kept her head held down waiting on her mother's conclusion when Josie said, "I should have thrown you away just like you did your kid!" with that, Josie stormed into her bedroom and slammed the door. Lillie had grown accustomed to the pain of her mother's rants but that last statement hurt Lillie more than anything she had ever felt in her life. *As Lillie sat there as the tears began to pour down her face, thinking, I didn't mean to hurt Diamond. I didn't know what to do, I was scared then, I've been scared my whole life. Lillie started to get angry at her mother. If Josie wasn't so upset and mad all of the time I would have been able to tell her I was pregnant. I would have been able to tell her I was raped by one of her male friends. If Josie cared about someone other than herself and had the sense to take her male friends elsewhere I wouldn't have been pregnant in the first place. I wanted to bring my baby home, but why bring a baby into a world where she could never be happy. I put my baby in a place where she could be loved, looked after and well taken care of. I watched my baby grow up, and she grew up fine. Curtis told me that my baby girl has become a successful businesswoman and she's making a lot of money. I wanted to be apart of my baby's life but you-Josie took that from me. So Josie, your life isn't the only life that was ruined.* Lillie was panting when she broke away from her thoughts. She so desperately wanted to tell her mother all of those things. She knew she couldn't, she didn't have the heart. Lillie felt like her mother had been hurt enough and she promised herself a long time ago she would never be the one to hurt her anymore than the world already had.

After going over company Business Diamond, Marshal and Teresa sat in Diamond's office around the round table. They all had earned more money than any of them knew what to do with. They all sat laughing and reflecting about how three years prior each of them were working at Smith and Smith's. Diamond threw the question of Hunter's Parts Plant on the table. She asked the pair if they knew anything about the company and why they had so many layoffs. "Yes I know that place my niece Lillie works there." Teresa said. "Well like my father she is probably laid off too. I want to find out more about this company and why they're having so many layoffs." Diamond stated. Marshal looked at Diamond and knew exactly where she was going with this. After working so closely with Diamond and truly getting to know her for the last few years he could read the ambition in her eyes. "Looks like you're planning to do some shaking up over there," Marshal said with a smile. "I'll check on it and get back to you." Marshal continued. He packed up his briefcase and exited the room. "And I'm gonna check on my niece, it's been a while. The only thing is she lives with my crazy sister, and after our mama died spending all of her years taking care of my sister's kids I didn't want to have anything to do with my sister," Teresa said. Diamond was confused she asked, "She can't be that bad?" "Please, you should see how she got my niece living like a slave. She never had a relationship or kids and my sister didn't even let her go to school. Now Lillie is a woman and walks around like a scared little girl," Teresa explained. Diamond felt sorry for Lillie, she began to think, *if it's that bad why won't Teresa help her?* Then there was a hard knock on the door it was Derrick. "What are you two beautiful ladies talking about in here?" Derrick asked with a fake grin. Teresa was smiling from ear to ear. "Oh, just girl talk," Teresa replied like a sixteen year old talking to her first crush. Teresa got up from her seat and walked out of the office with Derrick. Diamond could see how hard Teresa was falling for this man. Diamond was hoping and praying that Teresa didn't get hurt because there was something cunning about Derrick; Diamond could feel it and she didn't like it. But that was Teresa's personal business. As long as it didn't interfere with company business Diamond was going to keep her opinion to herself. "What you and the boss lady talk about Teresa, is it something I can get into?" Derrick asked. "We were talking about business, but with you I want to talk about pleasure . . . Are we still on for tonight?" Teresa smiled seductively. "For sure," Derrick said as the two walked to his office. *One day I'm going to be the top dog. Diamond is a smart woman and I want everything she has.* Derrick thought to himself.

A few days later Marshal told Diamond the Hunter's Part Plant was a family business and made parts for local car shops. The big heads of the company worked the employees twelve hours a day and Saturdays to create a surplus of product. Once the company reached a certain quota the company would lay off the majority of the laborers. When the supply stock ran low the company would call the workers back. There was no union system instituted in the company so there was no time and a half pay for the over worked employees. "Make an offer Marsh. I looked into the profit value and if we can take over we can expand to shops outside the local area. We can buy more equipment and open the company up to make more parts. Through the purchase of the equipment we can open the scope of the business and cater to a wider field of demand. We can also improve and update the parts the company is known for producing." Marshal and Diamond began to talk more and crunch numbers. Each made calls and had some strings pulled. The Hunter's Parts Plant was going into its fourth generation and they were ready to sell.

Diamond had to spend a lot of money for this plant but it was worth every penny. All the workers were called back to work and were gathered to see the new owner. Diamond walked in the building with her blue pinstripe two piece suit (one of her personal designs) looking sharp. She had Marshal standing next to her; she then took the platform above all of the workers. Diamond scanned her audience searching for her father. When she saw him he just happen to look up; their eyes connected. Curtis' mouth fell open; he was shocked to see his daughter announcing her ownership of the company. She was so beautiful and elegant standing high above the crowd. Her words were strong, direct and assertive. "There will be big changes being made here at this company. First there will be a human recourses department added to the team to make sure everyone is treated fairly. Second there are plans to expand and add more features to the company. This expansion project will insure each individual position and make promotions available. There will be no more layoffs if possible and anyone interested in training for the new equipment is welcome. Third my favorite part of all, and I'm sure you'll all like this part, time and a half will be paid for all overtime. Everyone was shouting and clapping. Diamond winked at her father. Curtis was so proud, he wanted to tell everyone she was his daughter but he knew that would change how his coworkers thought of him. No one knew Diamond was his daughter except Lillie. Curtis looked around and saw Lillie in the corner all alone. She was smiling; her eyes were wide open. Curtis did a double take; he thought he was looking at an older version of Diamond. Then he thought, I wonder, *NO WAY! She couldn't be . . .* The hunter's plant was renamed Diamond's Parts. Just like she said the place was expanded and remodeled. She brought in new updated equipment and opened the company's spectrum. She sold to not only local dealers but globally marketed the products. She got more attention and sells than the former company could ever imagine. Before the year was out Diamond not only had the money she invested into back; she tripled it and opened up three other locations. At the next board meeting Diamond, Marshal, Teresa and the other board members, Rita, Cory, Juan, and Derrick discussed the new companies and reviewed the profits. The numbers didn't lie; sells were going through the roof. Diamond sat with a great feeling deep inside her. Her father was made supervisor and would never have to worry about being laid off. Diamond made plenty of money out of the deal and everyone congratulated her for taking such a risk and seizing a grand opportunity. Derrick came over to her and shook her hand; he held it a little longer than she liked and asked her if she needed any help with the company. Diamond yanked her hand away from his and told him she had it covered. Derrick walked away angry. He was jealous, she was making money and he wanted some of it if he could not have all of it.

Later Teresa invited Diamond to have dinner at her home, Diamond excepted happy to finally be away from business. Teresa was special to her, she looked up to Teresa like a mentor; there was a closeness Diamond felt between the two of them. "Diamond can I say something to you on a personal level?" Teresa said lowering her voice. Diamond wondered what she was going to say. Teresa didn't usually ask permission to give Diamond her opinion; she normally said what was on her mind. "I've watched you grow up into a big business woman in these last few years. I've grown close to you. You're like the daughter I never had. It's a feeling I didn't know I ever wanted. I watched my sister have so many kids at an early age and not ever finish high school. She never had a job, and she was always angry, mad and frustrated. I knew I didn't want that kind of life for myself. So I worked hard, and I gave up a lot of freedom and a big chunk of my private life. I filled my time with school and working my way up until now and now with your help I'm a successful black woman, but look at my house, listen at how quiet it is. I wish that I had a family to share my success with. The reason why I am saying this is I don't want you to end up like me. Don't let years go by and miss out on what's really important—a family!" Diamond took all of Teresa's advice to heart. When Diamond left she drove through the gates in her red Corvette to her big mansion. She sat and thought about what Teresa had said.

She was right, Diamond was a successful, beautiful, rich, black woman but deep down she was lonely. Diamond thought of her birth parents and if she had sisters or brothers. But like usual she dismissed the thought— Curtis and Beulah were the only parents she needed. Through all these daydreams the truth remained the same, Diamond ached for a man. Like Teresa, Diamond had passed up a lot of men to achieve her goal. Now that she had it, it was time to open her heart to someone. *The question is who? It is so hard to find someone who is not, caught up in all the money,* Diamond pondered. That night before Diamond got in her cold lonely bed, she prayed to the Lord to send a good man into her life.

CHAPTER 7

Where Is The Love?

The next morning at the office Marshal told Diamond there was a big business convention in California. He was going to fly over in the private plane he convinced Diamond to buy. She named it Diamond #5. Marshal advised Diamond to purchase the plane for their personal safety. Being so wealthy it was not safe to walk around like most people did. Diamond was finding out how people treated her differently. People constantly asked her for money, even people she didn't know. When she didn't give them what they asked for she was often times called stuck up or sell-out or even selfish, that hurt her the most. There were so many people that wanted her help, but when she offered them jobs they'd make an excuse for not being able to work. That upset Diamond; she had worked long and hard to get where she was while other people expected handouts. It got so bad to the point Diamond started going by Diane. She didn't want people to know who she was; that worked better for her. With the alias Diamond was able to really get to see the realness of people. She decided she would let Marshal be the face of Dcorp.

When Diamond and Marshal arrived at the grand hotel meeting area they were greeted with the highest respect. The majority of the companies representatives present at the meeting were hoping to launch joint ventures with Dcorp. A partnership with Dcorp meant stability and backing and all of the smaller companies wanted just that. As the meeting carried on in the ballroom there was, another smaller banquet room. This area was set up for families and personal conversations. After a couple of hours Diamond was tired and needed a break; she hadn't taken a vacation since the company opened. Marshal told her she should mingle and get to know some people. Diamond agreed but under one condition, she was going to mingle under her alias Diane and not her real name. When it was Dcorp.'s turn to be represented, Marshal approached the podium while Diamond watched in the crowd. Marshal was articulate and elegant in his presentation, Diamond was proud and confident in her partner, and her assistance was not needed.

Diamond slipped away to the smaller banquet hall trying her best to by pass all of the people who knew who she was. This task was not easy for the simple fact that there were very few black people and even fewer black women. Diamond managed to make it into the banquet room unrecognized. She took a seat in the corner of the room with her plate. Diamond checked out the scene, it was laid back and a lot less up tight. Sitting in the corner was okay for the first couple of minutes, and then it got kind of lonely. Diamond noticed a woman sitting at a table picking at her food; she had to be lonely and bored too. She was a small framed, brown skinned woman and she looked kind of familiar. It was obvious she had attended the meeting with her spouse who was most likely in the ballroom chatting with the other businessmen and viewing different company presentations. Diamond had nothing to lose so she got up and walked over to the woman. When the woman lifted her head it was Felisha Daniels—her best friend in high school.

"Felisha is that you?" Diamond asked excitedly. "Diamond girl what's up?" Felisha yelled. They hugged each other tight. "I go by Diane now," Diamond explained. "Oh because you think you grown now?" Felisha laughed, "Okay, Diane what you doing at his boring meeting?" Diamond remembered how close she and Felisha were in high school; and didn't want their relationship to change so she kept her secret. "I'm here scouting out some things for the company I work for." Diamond felt she was not lying because she was there for that very reason; she just left out the part that she was the owner. The two ladies talked and laughed. Diamond got a chance to really catch up with her friend. Felisha informed Diamond of her marriage to her husband Terrance Walker a top sales representative of Conners Appliance. (A private owned company Marshal thought had the ability of growing with good marketing and planning). Felisha told Diamond about her husband always working and the fact that his brother worked for the same company.

When the meeting was over and the rest of the group joined their families, Diamond had the opportunity to meet Felisha's husband. He was a tall dark brown skinned man, well built with a low faded hair cut. Diamond could tell he was a very serious business like brother but he liked to be called Terry away from the office. Diamond was kind of nervous, she was hoping and praying Terry did not recognize her face; when he didn't she was relieved. Felisha ragged on how awful the food was and suggested they all grab dinner somewhere else. Diamond was up for that idea she was ready to leave; she didn't want to discuss business at all she wanted to enjoy a normal conversation with Felisha. Diamond went to tell Marshal she was going out and her vacation started as of right then she let him know she had run into an old friend and was going to visit with her. That made Marshal happy to hear he was beginning to worry about Diamond. He saw that she was too young to be about business twenty-four hours of the day and have no personal life. They all had made a lot of money with Dcorp. The investments they had made were doing nothing but profiting. Yet and still Diamond had no children, or even a love life for that matter. Marshal knew Diamond would have a hard time finding a man. Very few men could handle such a confident, strong, powerful and intimidating woman. Marshal was glad Diamond was going to keep her identity a secret. He gave her his stamp of approval telling her to be careful and have fun. Diamond rode back with Terry and Felisha. Diamond was glad to see Felisha had found happiness with her husband and her two children Carrie eight and Terry Jr. six. Watching Felisha also made her sad; with all the money she had, if she were to pass away the next day there would be no one to leave it to. True enough she had her parents and her brother Dennis, but no children of her own to inherit her fortune. Diamond had placed Dennis over Diamond Part Plant, that gave him and her father a chance to grow closer and Beulah was overjoyed to see that also. Beulah was also proud to see her Diamond in the ruff shine. All of that was good but Diamond felt like she needed more in her life.

When the three of them got to the house Diamond felt so comfortable. Felisha and her husband lived in a cute, clean, three-bedroom home. Felisha showed Diamond around she was introduced to the couple's children as well as two of their nieces. There was Tasha a small framed, brown skin fifteenyear-old and her sister Chantel who looked similar at only seven years old. Tasha had a bit of an attitude Diamond noticed that right away. Diamond picked that up in her conversation; she was feisty. Tasha was saying if her dad didn't make it there on time, she was going to walk home because she was ready to go. The girls lived miles away so walking would have been a true act of her determination. While the two ladies talked Felisha began to cook dinner. Diamond offered to help and was a little hurt when Felisha declined. Diamond wanted to show her cooking expertise. When she was young Beulah taught her how to cook but this was Felisha's house and she was enjoying her hospitality. Chantel confidently walked in the kitchen, she was on a quest for information. She wanted to know who this pretty lady sitting in her aunt's kitchen was. Chantel was a talker; Felisha was shocked to see how much patience Diamond had with her. Felisha didn't expect that from a woman with no children of her own. Diamond was feeling good. This was better than conquering a big business deal, or even purchasing another company. In the process of Chantel's questioning, the doorbell rang.

Terry opened the door and there standing on the front porch was his brother Quenton Walker. Quenton was a tall thirty three-year-old man with a chocolate brown complexion. He was well groomed with his short hair cut and neatly trimmed mustache. He had a body that could easily be recognized through his tight shirt. His arms were big and strong and his six pack was packing. He was there to pick up his daughters. When he walked into the house he heard Chantel talking away as she normally did, but he also heard an unfamiliar voice responding. Quenton walked into the kitchen to investigate. There he found Chantel having a conversation with a beautiful black sister. Diamond was looking good. She had a nice sophisticated lavender suit, her hair was flat ironed straight hanging passed her shoulders and her face was made up in soft, subtle tones which accented her natural beauty. *Wow! Quenton thought, who is this fine sistah spending time with my daughter? It touched his heart to watch them. When Diamond looked up at this fine brother standing in the doorway she was immediately attracted to him. Look at that smile, so wide and bright, she thought. Her eyes are so inviting, Quenton thought.*

They both stared at each other totally in a daze. Chantel snapped them back to reality when she bolted from her seat to her father. She hugged him, grabbed his hand and led him to Diamond. Chantel told her dad, "Daddy, this is Miss. Diane," she pointed at her father and continued, "Miss. Diane, this is daddy." Felisha laughed and let Diamond know his name was Quenton and he was Terry's brother. Diamond rose up from her seat to shake his hand. When she touched his hand there was a warm tingling all over her body. Diamond listened attentively as he further introduced himself. The entire time he spoke Diamond's heart was pounding. She was afraid he could see it through her blazer jacket. This man was sexy, she was so excited but she played it cool, she didn't want to look like a schoolgirl with her first crush. The two talked more with Chantel and Felisha. Felisha could feel the vibe between Diamond and Quenton and asked if he'd like to stay for dinner. In Quenton's mind he wanted to stay and spend time getting to know "Diane" but his heart wouldn't allow it. *"You know you're not ready to put yourself out there to get hurt again" His heart told him.* Quenton could feel his attraction growing for Diamond more and more with every moment he spent with her. *You know this lady here is not your average woman, you know you ain't ready for that—not right now,* his conscience told him. He didn't have to worry about declining dinner because Tasha charged into the kitchen and announced she was ready to go right then. She had her coat and walked out the door and went to sit in the car. Quenton apologized for his daughter's behavior, said his good byes and left with his girls. "Felisha I don't mean to get into Quenton's business, but can I ask? What's his story?" Diamond asked. "Di, Quenton has had hard times taking care of his daughters all by himself. I know you noticed he didn't have a wedding ring on. Well that's because he married this tramp who did him wrong. They got a divorce and he took the children and been trying to raise them on his own for the last five years. He's been working at the plant long hours and the girls spend most of their time at their grandparent's house. That's why Tasha is so hard, she's mad at her mother and father." Diamond sat and thought about the situation, *a man with baggage, that's too bad . . .* It was always like that. Every time she was interested in getting to know someone they would go crazy when they found out who she really was or have some type of baby-mama-drama to deal with. Diamond was not getting involved with any of that. *What a shame, I was kind of liking him.* After a wonderful dinner and more hours of talking it was time for Diamond to go back to the hotel. Felisha tried to get her to stay at her house, Diamond was moved by the offer; someone was trying to do something for her just for the sake of being nice—Diamond hadn't experienced that in a long time, most people were trying to get something from her. She was sad she had to decline the offer but she let Felisha know she would be in town for a week. Felisha told her she was going to take her around town. Diamond took a cab back to the hotel then she got back to her room and got on her cell phone and called Marshal. She told him she was very interested in the Connors Appliance Plant. As she laid down to sleep she realized she couldn't get Quenton out of her mind.

CHAPTER 8

Betrayal

After getting the girls home and eating another McDonald's meal and dealing with Tasha's attitude and Chantel's hunger for attention Quenton was tired. The girls were finally sleeping and now it was his turn. Quenton laid down but couldn't get to sleep. He stared at the ceiling. He turned over on his side and imagined fine Diane lying in the empty spot next to him. He smiled then another vision came to mind. It was Mira—his ex-wife and the reason for all the turmoil in the house now.

As he thought back when they were in high school he was the popular kid, good looking, and fine, as the girls would say. He was the captain of the basketball team and an A student. He had scholarships from everywhere all the colleges wanted him on their team. In college he was going to major in business following after his older brother Terry. Terry was already in college. Like Diamond in many ways, Quenton had plans to be in the big business world. He had so many options and opportunities, which made his parents Ray and Sara proud. His younger brother Quincy and his twin Laura Lee were right behind him.

At sixteen he had it all, his family, school and his best friend Ernest Reed. Ernest was the same age as Quenton and since grade school they were close. They were always together, on the same basketball teams, and going for the same major. Only Ernest wasn't as handsome as Quenton, Ernest was medium height, medium weight, light skinned and when it came to his face he was just okay, he had no flare to his look, he was average. Because of this he didn't get as many girls as Quenton. He was not as smart as Quenton either so he didn't have as many scholarships offer's either. And because of this Ernest started to have this under cover jealousy of his best friend he could not shake. Ernest couldn't help it so he kept it hidden because if Quenton got something he knew he would share with him and hook him up.

When they were both seventeen they both went to a house

party and met Mira. Mira went to another high school and right away Ernest wanted her. She was dark skinned with big lips and hips and all the guys were after her. Everyone except Quenton who was too busy talking to all the other girls Ernest approached Mira and threw all the game he could at her and was still shot down. Embarrassment turned into rage when Ernest watched as Mira slipped between Quenton and another girl to get his attention. Mira was spicy and sassy, what she wanted she got and what she wanted was Quenton. Quenton was not interested in her, it didn't take long to see that she was too aggressive for him, so he listen to her try to get with him, but brushed her off but Mira was not taking no for an answer. She spat her charm and threw her sex appeal on him and yet he still brushed her off. Ernest was happy to see Quenton walk away from Mira; but he was still jealous how Mira wanted Quenton and not him. The party went on and after another hour Quenton and Ernest left. Mira not giving up on Quenton asked around and found out where he went to school.

Then one afternoon while some of the fellows were playing ball outside at school Mira showed up. She was dressed to impress, she wore skintight jeans, her make-up was flawless and her long weave not only gorgeous-it was perfect. She turned everybody's head; the guys playing ball were gawking with their tongue hanging out. Mira walked straight up to Quenton and he looked around to see the reaction of everyone surrounding him. He saw that all the guys were watching, and watching hard, that's when Quenton felt like he was the man. Quenton pulled Mira aside and talked with her for little a while. Ernest watched the whole scenario from a distance. He was steaming, he wanted Mira and he was going to get her. He didn't know how but he was going to have her for himself. Ernest knew today nor the next would be the day and after two weeks of Quenton and Mira hanging out and Quenton leaving him hanging he began to seriously hate Quenton. Ernest bottled it up and began throwing doubt in Quenton's ear. He would tell Quenton, Mira wasn't good enough for him, or he would say she wasn't the one. Quenton wasn't stupid, he knew he didn't want to spend the rest of his life with her but for the time being she was fun, pretty and sexy; the big head had nothing to do with Mira and Quenton's relationship, the little head had total control of their arrangement. At that age he thought he was invincible, that's why he was having sex with Mira without a condom. In his defense she did tell him she was on the pill after a few months later Mira told Quenton she was pregnant. Quenton was shocked, discussed and frustrated. Mira told him she must have missed some days taking her pills and that's how it happened. Quenton's parents were broken hearted. They didn't care too much for Mira because she was disrespectful, she would call at all hours of the night, come in their house and not speak, and last but not least there was the clincher; Quenton's parents were Christian people and Mira refused to go to church with them. They knew they didn't want her as a daughter-in-law. Unfortunately Quenton was stuck between a rock and a hard place. He wanted to go to college, take his brother's classes and find a good paying job. That's what he wanted but then Mira dropped out of school and her mother was throwing her out of their house. Her mother wanted Mira to go to school and take care of her child but her mother knew Mira and knew the baby would slowly but surely be her responsibility. So Quenton convinced his parents to allow Mira to stay with them. Even though Mira was pregnant she went out and partied just about every night up until her last month. Mira was the worst house guest, she would come home at all hours of the night, she was lazy, she didn't clean at all, and she wouldn't cook, and would holler and curse at Quenton the nights she wasn't out partying. It got so bad they had to move out. Then Mira and Quenton moved into a small apartment. Quenton had to drop out of school and get a job once Tasha was born. Quenton's mother helped out a lot she took care of the baby more than Mira. Mira was too busy running the streets to dedicate her time to her child. Quenton would come home to their small one bedroom apartment in the poorest, slum in town depressed. After working twelve hours a day at the dirty vegetable factory all Quenton wanted was to sit in a clean house with food on the table. With Mira that would never happen the apartment didn't take much to clean but Mira was too lazy to do anything other than party. She wouldn't get a job; she wouldn't watch the baby because she slept all the time. Often times Quenton would come home and find Tasha in her crib, wet, hungry and crying while Mira did nothing. Quenton couldn't handle the child neglect, so he dropped the baby off with his mother every morning when he went to work and picked her up when he got off, Mira loved that. Every time Quenton tried to talk to Mira she would throw in his face how she put her life on hold to have his baby. That's when Quenton would feel guilty, but he knew his life wasn't going the way he thought it should either. First he loved his child, but Mira wouldn't have been his choice as a wife but he felt he had to do the right thing for his child. Quenton married Mira and got his GED and landed a job at Conners Appliances with his brother Terry and best friend Ernest. They were made managers and when he got there it didn't take long before he was promoted to plant supervisor. Quenton was in charge of production in the plant. He organized the people, he ran the floor, and he made sure everything got done on the ground floor. The top floor was the business sector of the company. With Quenton's promotion he was making more money and decided to buy a three-bedroom home for his family. Mira had just had Chantel, their second child so he believed three bedrooms should be sufficient for them all. Quenton loved his two girls he vowed he'd never leave them. No matter how hard it was to live with Mira he was going to be with his girls.

After having Chantel the sex had dwindled down to once every few months and it wasn't enjoyable to either. It was only sex; there was no love involved. Mira never changed, she continued to do nothing: no cooking and cleaning was out of the question, all she did was sleep all day, and party all night. Quenton got used to this, so did the girls; they would eat most of their meals at Quenton's parents' house. He would work long hours stop by his parent's house to pick up his girls and head home. The time Mira would be at home, she would interact with the girls, but it wasn't enough. Tasha was a small girl, she really needed Mira, and it would hurt her when Mira was too tired to talk or play with her. She would cry when Mira was gone; Quenton tried to bring this issue to Mira's attention but she was not trying to hear anything that reflected her awful parenting skills. Quenton was frustrated; he couldn't spend the time like he wanted to with the girls because he had to work to put food on the table and clothes on their backs. He was doing okay with that, they weren't starving and the bills got paid, but Mira was not satisfied. She thought Quenton was going to be a rich man; at this point she was only getting by. She couldn't spend money like she wanted to; she would throw that fact in Quenton's face. He wouldn't argue with her in front of the girls, he would just walk away and wonder why Mira couldn't change for the sake of the girls. Mira did change. She changed for the very worst. Sometimes she wouldn't come home until the wee hours of the morning. Quenton wanted to knock some sense into her but he was taught better than that. Instead he would just bite his lip and go on. Then Quenton remembered one time at the company's annual family picnic Mira was smiling and flirting in Ernest's face. Ernest was loving it. He finally felt superior, he was Quenton's boss and he was working on the top floor and Quenton's wife wanted him. Ernest had a huge house, a few cars and wore expensive suits. He bragged on and on about how much money he made.

"I don't know bro but it looks like your boss is trying to step up to your wife," Quincy said. Quincy was a smooth dark brown, clean—bald-headed with a goatee, fine built, sharp as a tack brother. He was street smart and people smart; and when he saw Mira and Ernest in the back talking and laughing he tried to warn Quenton. Quenton only replied was, "Listen Q, I know Mira ain't all that trust worthy, but Ernest, that's my boy from way back and I trust him with my life." "Go ahead and trust him with your life, because it's your wife that he wants. You better open up your eyes bro," Quincy expressed. Quenton didn't respond; he couldn't and wouldn't believe either one of them would do him that way. Soon after the picnic Ernest was having Quenton stay and work longer hours at the plant. Quenton couldn't leave unless either he or Ernest was there to take care of a problem. This went on for weeks; until one day Quenton got a call to pick up Tasha from school. She was sick and the school couldn't get through to Mira. Quenton told Terry the situation, Terry took over for him while he left to see about his child. After picking Tasha up and Chantel who was at his parent's home Quenton drove home with a funny feeling in his stomach, something was not right. Quenton thought Mira probably came home and passed out and didn't hear the phone ring. As Quenton got closer to the house the feeling got stronger and stronger. Then he got to their street, from the end of the block he could see Ernest's shiny BMW parked Quenton knew Ernest license plate number. Anger crept up his spine. Quenton was hurt and he hoped and prayed that this situation wasn't the way it looked. When Quenton drove up to the house he told Tasha to stay in the car for a minute he then walked in his house in over to his bedroom and heard the familiar sound of people having sex. Quenton was hot; he stood outside the door, thinking. If I don't leave now I'm going to kill both of them. He turned to leave and stopped dead in his tracks. Rage had replaced the hurt inside of him; he was ready to erupt like a volcano. He said out loud, "Oh HELL, NAW!" He kicked the door so hard it came off the hinges. There they were, Mira and Ernest, butt naked in his bed. Both of the guilty counterparts jumped up and stared at Quenton standing in the doorway. They were terrified, neither one knew what he was about to do. All Quenton could think about was hurting both of them, then he thought of his girls sitting in the car waiting on daddy. Quenton took a deep breath and with all the self control he could gather up said, "If it wasn't for the fact that I got my two little girls out there waiting for me, you both would be dead. Mira, when I get back you better have all your shit and be outta this house, and you Ernest," Quenton looked him squarely in the eyes. Quenton had to contain himself from doing what he wanted to do. Quenton took another deep breath and continued his statement, "You were my friend, my best friend, you were like a brother to me, and then you come and do this to me? After all the times I stood up for your ass. How stupid I was to not believe what people said about you. They told me you were a dog, but no, I'm not going to whoop your ass. No bro, I'm gonna do worse, I'm gonna give you this tramp. All of her take her! This way you two won't have to sneak around like the snakes you are!" With that Quenton walked out the house and left. Quenton drove around for hours trying to calm himself down; The girls had fallen asleep in the backseat so Quenton found a place to park with a view of the city lights. Quenton watched his beautiful daughters resting peacefully. They were so innocent, kind and sweet. Looking down on them he remembered his vow to them. He would take care of them always and be there for them.

Things didn't turn out the way Mira had hoped when she moved out. She tried to go with Ernest but he told her he didn't want her. "I hope you feel the same way I did when you shot me down in the beginning!" He said. Mira had no other choice but to go back and stay with her mother. And soon got hooked on drugs Quenton divorced her and was awarded sole custody of their two children. After the order Mira made no attempt to see the girls. The divorce took a major toll on Tasha. She wanted to at least see her mother. She wanted to know where she was and what she was doing; all of these unanswered questions made her an angry young girl. Quenton tried to keep things together, but he was also angry and hurt. He had to play daddy and mommy, and go to work and face a boss he wanted to beat up every time he saw him. Quenton wasn't going to let Ernest take his wife and his job; his girls had to eat. Quenton swallowed his pride and showed up everyday and preformed to the best of his ability.

After five years Quenton still wasn't ready for a real relationship with a woman. Mira had tricked him, shamed him, cheated on him, and stomped on his heart so bad; he promised himself he would never allow that to happen again. Now his life was totally dedicated to taking care of his kids and making it in the business world. Quenton wanted to go further in his company but he didn't see it happening; so he tried other avenues. He started a singing group with his brother Quincy, Sister Laura Lee, and Cousin Mark. Mark was the group's lead singer; he had swagger with his golden brown complexion, short fade, medium built body, family facial features and charm. And he could sing the panties off women. With their group holding down a perfect harmony and flare Quenton could see they were going places. Quenton hoped the first place they went was far from Conners Appliances. Quenton was the group's self proclaimed manager, he worked during the day at Connor's to keep food and shelter for his girls and long hours during the night trying to make this group thing work. As far as his love life . . . that was put on hold, until he could learn to trust a woman and love her but his heart was cold until today, he thought, then he saw Miss Diane and the more he thought about her he had to get up and take a cold shower to cool him down.

CHAPTER 9

Family Affair

When Diamond woke up in a huge bed in her luxury hotel room she felt refreshed. She walked around her presidential suite looking out of the windows taking in sunny California. Diamond was so relaxed, she sat on the comfortable sofa with a cup of coffee clearing her mind of numbers, charts and percents. Right in Diamonds moment of complete peace, her cell phone rang. "Girl get up! I'm coming to get you" Felisha said. Diamond jumped up happy as if she had a new life. She dressed as quickly as she could and flew down the hall to the elevator to meet Felisha in the lobby. Felisha had dropped the kids off with Terry's parents and was going to have a girl's day out. After picking up Diamond they went to Laura Lee's house to pick her up.

Laura Lee was a pretty faced, full figured woman, with a big blonde weave, a few gold teeth and long painted finger nails full of designs. When she got in the car she started talking. Boy could she talk, she talked about anything and everything; she was loud and spicy. Diamond liked her right away because she was real. She was Laura Lee whether you like it or not. The three ladies had a ball. Felisha took them to stores to shop. She worked at a fashion boutique so she knew exactly where to go to find the good stuff. Diamond thought it was funny because one of the shops they'd gone into carried her personal line. Felisha told Diamond that some people had clothes designs with her name on them. "Girl remembers when we wanted to design clothes we were so young, well at least I got to work in the store, and this new line of Diamond Fashions is selling out as soon as it hits the rack. The stuff is cute but it ain't as good as the stuff we used to come up with," Felisha laughed. Diamond laughed and agreed.

Going in and out of the shops made Laura Lee hungry, she was ready to grub. "Let's go to mama's house," she said. When the ladies got to the house there was an older couple sitting in the living room. Sara and Ray Walker were in their late sixties. There were also four children in the living room, Terry and Felisha's two, Carrie and Terry Jr. as well as Quenton's two, Tasha and Chantel. When Chantel saw Diamond she jumped up to hug her. The adults were shocked to see how well Chantel had taken to 'Miss. Diane'. Tasha had disappeared, Diamond wondered where she had gone; Diamond could sense a pain deep inside the young girl. After Diamond introduced herself to Ray and Sara they saw what Chantel saw, a beautiful, smart, friendly respectful woman. Felisha told the couple how she was showing 'Diane' around. Sara asked 'Diane' what she had liked best about her tour. Diamond told her everything was good but she would like to visit a church. Even though Diamond was a rich businesswoman she tried to make it to church every Sunday. Diamond knew it was God that got her where she was. The couple's eyes lit up when they heard Diamond mention church. "Well Sunday morning you can hang with the saints, but tonight you going out with the aint's!" Laura Lee said. Everybody fell out laughing, even Ray and Sara. Sara realized that it was wrong to laugh and promote worldly behavior so she collected herself and said, "Now Laura, don't run her off. Would you like to have Dinner with us?" Diamond said she'd love to.

The crowd migrated to the dining room, and there he was—OH WOW, Diamond thought. They stood in the center of the room staring at each other. Laura Lee and Quincy looked at them and then at each other. Then Laura Lee said "Q, you got a penny for their thoughts?" Quincy responded, "Sis I'm gonna need my check book to cover all them thoughts." Quincy laughed, and then both of them laughed out loud, which broke the hold. Both Diamond and Quenton were embarrassed; they were caught in the moment. As everyone attempted to take their place at the table Quincy and Laura did some hustling and took the free seats forcing Diamond to sit right next to Quenton. Quincy then gave Laura and Felisha a wink. At first both Quenton and Diamond were nervous because they could feel the physical attraction, but after a while they loosened up. Everyone laughed and ate Diamond noticed Laura and Quincy was the type of twins that liked to argue and debate with one another. It was fun listening to them Diamond was overwhelmed she was surrounded by genuine people who were lively, loving and sincere the joy Diamond felt was priceless. After eating a great meal Laura told Diamond she was taking her to the Hot Spot, a hip-hop spot in the middle of the city. Quenton and Felisha gave Laura a strange look. "What are you looking at me like that for?" she asked. "That place is not suitable for a nice respectable lady like Diane," Quenton said. "Oh Quenton, I recall seeing you there a few times," Quincy said with his face fixed in a sly smile. Everyone burst out laughing, including Diamond. Diamond thought it was cute that Quenton was concerned about where she went. "Well don't worry Di, I got your back," Laura assured Diamond. "Yeah she'll have your back, way back in the corner with some dude" Quincy interjected. Quenton nodded his head in agreement.

That night while Diamond dressed to go out Marshal called alerting Diamond of the open Conners Appliances shares. A lot of the shareholders didn't see the companies profit and were willing to sell—for cheap. Diamond asked how much was available, Marshal informed her he had spoken to Fred Conners the owner of the company and he had forty shares. Diamond thought about it, the fact that Felisha, Terry and Quenton all had their livelihood based on that company swayed her to take initiative. She gave Marshal the go a head to place an offer on 51% of the company. Marshal knew how to negotiate and Diamond knew he would make the right moves. Her mind was clear of the business stuff for the time being now she was going out, when she got back she and Marshal would put their heads together and find a way to pull the company off the floor. But tonight was Miss. Diane's night to let loose, but not before she called her parents.

Curtis answered the phone, he talked and talked, Beulah was gone to church. Curtis made it clear that everything was running smoothly. He told Diamond the company was doing well and Dennis was doing a fine job keeping things rolling. He also let her know that he was going to pick an assistant and he thought about selecting a sweet lady named Lillie to help him. She was a hard worker, she was always on time, she did a good job, and she was quiet and shy, according to Curtis. "You know her sweetie, she's your old friend Cindy's older sister. Diamond raked her mind for a minute or two. Then it came to her. She remembered the timid woman that never looked anyone in the eyes. She remembered having to strain herself to hear her when she spoke. "Yeah Daddy, I'm sure she's a nice lady but I don't think that would be a good position for her. And I don't think she would want it either." Curtis agreed. In his mind he still felt someone should still do something nice for her.

Meanwhile that night back at home, Teresa and Derrick had been going out spending a lot of time together. They decided to go out to dinner, when they entered the restaurant Teresa let out a sigh of disgust. "What's wrong baby?" Derrick asked. "There's my sorry sister sitting over there with my nieces, Lillie and Cindy," Teresa hissed. "Lets go, I don't want to see Josie." Teresa turned toward the door; Cindy spotted her and called over to her. "Oh shit!" Teresa said then Teresa and Derrick walked over to the table Josie looked at Derrick like he was a piece of meat and she was hungry. Teresa didn't see the look or she would have never sat down to join them. She tried her best to be cordial and mask her dislike for Josie in front of her nieces, especially Lillie. It hurt Teresa to see Lillie had grown up and never shook the scared little girl phase. Lillie was middle aged, not a bad looking woman and still could not project her voice and stand up for herself. Teresa was lost in her thought, when she snapped back to reality she was caught off guard she was looking at Lillie and could swear she saw Diamond. It was kind of weird, they looked so much a like but their personalities were exact opposite. Poor Lillie never had a man or a life because of this creature Teresa that was now looking at-Josie. Josie was smiling and grinning at Derrick. Derrick thought Josie was attractive but she was beneath him. She didn't look like she had much money and he didn't date poor women. "Aunt Teresa what you been doing lately?" Cindy asked. "I'm working along with Derrick at Diamond Corporations," Teresa replied. "I know Diamond, I went to school with her and Grandma took us to church with her and her parents Curtis and Beulah." Teresa mentioned that she had met Diamond's parents and they were good people. "Yeah but they're not her real parents, they adopted her. No one knows who her real parents are. All they know is that she was left at the Bradford's house in their backyard on a garbage can. But look at her now, I know if I were her mama I'd be kicking my own ass," Cindy laughed. Josie listen closely all while Cindy spoke. When Cindy mentioned the garbage can Josie started calculating the ages. When she figured it out she started to choke.

Diamond, the multi-million dollar businesswoman was Lillie's child! "It was probably some young girl that didn't have good guidance at home," Teresa said "How do you know Teresa? You think you know everything. You so high and mighty that you think you're so smart, you make me sick!" Josie yelled. Teresa got up from the table to avoid making a scene. She grabbed her purse, took Derrick's arm all while Josie expressed the pleasure it was to meet him. Josie gave him a seductive wink and smiled while Derrick escorted Teresa out thinking, if she wasn't poor I might have let her have some. Lillie sat with her head hung low sad now her mother had found out about her daughter and she hated to hear her mother go off on her Aunt Teresa. Aunt Teresa was always nice to her and during hard times she would slip Lillie money. Lillie never had to ask for help; some how her Aunt always knew when she needed a little boost to make ends meet. "Mama why are you always arguing with Aunt Teresa?" Cindy asked. "Look, you asked me and Lillie to come to this place. I didn't come here to listen to miss perfect. I've had to live with that shit all while we were growing up. Not anymore. Now why don't you go get me some cigarettes baby" Josie said trying to get Cindy to leave. When Cindy was a safe distance from the table Josie was bouncing with excitement. "Lillie, Lillie!" Lillie was scared, she thought she had somehow made her mother upset. "Lillie, that woman Diamond . . . That's your daughter!" Lillie never lifted her head, "I know mama." "What? You mean to tell me we've been struggling poor all this time and your daughter is so stinking rich she owns her own plane and we don't even have a car? How could you?" Josie said. She was about to lay the guilt trip on Lillie but had to discontinue the mind control because Cindy was approaching the table. "This isn't over, we'll talk more about this when we get home," Josie mumbled. A tear rolled down Lillie's face. She had prayed this day would never come and here she was and her daughter was exposed to her mother. Nothing would be the same.

That night Diamond and Laura Lee walked into the Hot Spot both dressed to kill. Laura wore a short glitter dress and Diamond wore tight black leather pants with a gold and black top she'd designed. Passing through the entrance and getting a good look at the dance floor Diamond could see this was nothing like the places she had visited before. But then again she didn't get out much at all so it was interesting. Laura Lee was so funny and everyone seemed to know and like her. She was being hugged and greeted by just about everybody. When the fellows tried to come up to Diamond she told them to step off. Like Quincy, Laura saw a spark between Diamond and Quenton. Laura saw a glow in her brother's eyes, a glow she hadn't seen in years. The whole family loved and supported Quenton; he had it rough, it was time for him to be happy and live again. There was a unanimous vote for Diamond to be the woman to change his life around.

The ladies made their way to a back booth where they could talk. Laura had three rum and cokes to Diamond's one margarita. Diamond was amazed to see how well Laura handled her liquor; she was relaxed and attentive. They talked about a lot of things. Diamond told Laura all she did was work, go to church, visit with family, and that she didn't have a man. Well, we're gonna fix that baby girl, Laura Lee thought to herself. Laura proved to be a really good listener as Diamond went on. Then something caught both of the women's attention, just in time to see Quincy and Quenton walk in. They were both looking good and the women were throwing themselves in their path as they made their way through the crowd. "Look at those chicken heads ready to start clucking after my brothers," Laura Lee chuckled. Diamond's eyes followed Quenton from the door to his seat at the bar. Quincy sat down for a few seconds then saw some woman he wanted to put the Mack game to. Diamond smiled as she watched Quenton turn down all the women that approached him. For some reason she had a spark of energy, a light of confidence. She decided to try her luck and go ask him to dance. Laura Lee told her to go get him. Diamond snuck up behind him and asked in the sexiest voice she could conjure up, "Can I buy you a drink?" Quenton turned to decline but when he saw it was Diane his whole demeanor changed. "Are you trying to pick me up?" Quenton smiled. "Is it working?" Diamond smiled back. "I'm afraid it is," he said. They talked and laughed both feeling comfortable, excited and happy to be around each other. Diamond couldn't take her eyes off of Quenton his smile melted her heart. She had never felt like this before, it was scary in a way. Quenton was lost in Diamond's eyes and taken by her charm; she was so beautiful inside and out. Laura Lee and Quincy watched Diamond and Quenton from the back table, they slapped fives and gave the official fist bump, their plan to hook the two up was working. Diamond loved how Quenton's smile brightened his entire face, and then suddenly his expression changed. Diamond tried to figure out what happened. She turned and saw a dark skinned woman walk in with a short, low cut dress with her breast hanging out; she looked like she was poured in to the dress. All of the men were looking except Quenton. He turned his head and looked down at the bar. "What's wrong Quenton?" Diamond asked. Quenton looked up and gazed into Diamond's shiny sparkling eyes; he wasn't going to let Mira ruin this for him. "Can I take you somewhere a little bit quieter?" he asked. Diamond then told Laura Lee she was leaving with Quenton. Once Diamond got inside Quenton's car it all hit her at once—she was going on a date. Quenton was nervous too he hadn't gone out that much, alone with a woman since the divorce. Diamond hadn't been on a real date since the company opened. This was surreal for the both of them. Quenton was afraid he might get hurt again or worse disrupt his family. He looked over at Diamond in the passenger seat and knew she was worth a chance. "You want to talk about why you changed up in front of that lady?" Diamond quizzed. "Diane, I'm not gonna fake with you. I like you and I want to spend time with you, so I'm gonna be honest with you. The woman at the club was my ex-wife Mira. The girl's mother. It was a bad marriage and I've been raising the girls all alone since the divorce. She doesn't call, stop by or check on the girls. I kind of like that but I know it's hard for the girls sometimes. This is the first time in a very long time that I have even had a woman in my car other than my sister and I can't remember the last time I've been on a date. I know we just met but I haven't been this happy in a long time. I'm putting this out because I'm real and I want you to know about me and I want to know about you." Diamond sat there going back and forth in her mind, this is the time I'm supposed to be honest and tell the truth about who I am but I can't. If I tell him I won't really get a chance to get to know him like I want to. I like him but I know if I tell him he would think different of me. Diamond decided not to mention her wealth to Quenton.

Quenton then took Diamond to a fancy club; it was dark and romantic inside. It was beautifully decorated with flowers and candles. Diamond wished the night would never end, but after talking until closing time Quenton had to take her back to her hotel. He wanted to walk her up to her room, but no way could Diamond let him see she was staying in the presidential suite. Then she would have to explain, that would ruin the night, she couldn't do that. Quenton walked her to the elevator and kissed her softly on the cheek. It was so sweet she felt it deep inside of her; they made a date for the next day. As Diamond rode up the elevator she got misty eyed, she felt so good. Diamond couldn't wait until morning. Quenton was special, he kept racing through her mind, and he gave her feelings that no other man had ever given her.

When morning crept up Diamond wanted to make sure she looked extra gorgeous. Diamond put on one of her designs, it was a sleeveless tan shirt with designs and a pair of tight tan mid-length shorts that came down just above the knees, and she wanted to showcase her flawless legs. When Diamond walked out to the car Quenton was standing there waiting in his two piece brown printed outdoor outfit. He smiled at what he saw, and she did the same. Quenton took Diamond on a boat ride; that was her first time and sitting close to him and the water was strong yet calm, the steady flow of the waves was so romantic. Following the boat ride the pair grabbed some lunch and headed to the park where they sat and talked. Diamond listened as Quenton told her about the singing group he put together. He told her about his dream of being just like his brother Terry, he wished he could have the same position at work but there were only two spots and his ex-best friend had the other one. Quenton found it so easy to talk to 'Diane' he felt like he could tell her anything and everything except, the Mira and Ernest situation he wasn't quite ready to voice that yet. After going to a few more sights Quenton took Diamond to his parent's house for dinner. It was kind of like a tradition, just about all of the kids had dinner at Ray and Sara's house almost every evening. Quenton went faithful because he couldn't cook and had to pick his girls up anyway. Laura Lee and Quincy were both single and they knew their mother cooked as if they had never moved out.

As Diamond and Quenton walked through the door Tasha greeted Diamond with the rolling of her eyes, sucking of her teeth and her dramatic exit of the room. Quenton tried to play off his daughter's rudeness, but still Diamond could feel the pain inside of this girl. Everyone sat down talked and ate. Sara was extremely happy to see her son smiling again. It had been along time since the last time he had done so. Sara had prayed someone would put that joy back in her son. She prayed for a woman that could love him and his girls and take care of them. She was hoping Diane was the one. When Quenton took Diamond back to her hotel he asked her if he could walk her up to her room. Diamond politely refused, it wasn't time to expose herself, no not yet. The next morning Felisha, Terry and the kids picked Diamond up for church. It was a medium sized church holding around two hundred people. They got there early because Felisha was on the praise team. A little later Ray and Sara came in and soon after that Quenton and Chantel came in. Chantel sat in between Diamond and Quenton. It felt so right to Quenton; it felt like he had a complete family. He was impressed to see how well Chantel took to Diamond. As the service went on the praise team was doing their job, Diamond was up on her feet clapping and praising. Ray, sitting next to Quenton leaned over to him and said, "If she can cook you better get her." Quenton just smiled at his father. After church everyone did what they normally did—go to Ray and Sara's house for dinner. As they were eating nDiamond said Sara cooked so well she ought to have her own restaurant. Everyone got quiet. Diamond feeling confused didn't know what she had said or done wrong. Terry explained to Diamond, both Sara and Ray worked in a top restaurant bringing in a lot of customers using their own recipes. When the restaurant got big and they got older Sara and Ray were let go. Diamond felt bad but the businesswoman in her came out. "Then why don't you start your own restaurant?" "We've been trying to get that together, and get the group to start touring but it takes finances and commitment," Quenton said looking at Laura Lee and Quincy. "What you looking at me for?!" Laura Lee asked. "Because we can't tour if we can't get the singers to cooperate," Quincy said. "Oh no you didn't just go there Quincy! You the one who always be having us late waiting on you! And Quenton you ain't got to ride on that raggedy bus across the country with your butt sore from sitting on them hard seats!" Laura Lee shot back. "Well with all that butt you got it shouldn't be too bad," Quincy cracked. "YO MAMA!" Laura Lee shouted. Sara looked at Laura Lee as if she had lost her mind. After Sara's awkward pause everyone burst out laughing. Terry told Diamond the family has meetings discussing projects but it just the men. "What?" Diamond asked. "How is it a family meeting without the whole family?" "Because they stupid men," Laura Lee interjected. Terry pointed at Laura Lee and said, "That's why." Everyone laughed. In the back of her mind she thought, some men don't think women can handle business. If they knew now at thirty she was one of the most powerful black women around. Diamond had companies, stocks, her own clothing line and millions of dollars stored away and more coming in, it was too bad she couldn't tell them and prove them wrong about the women involvement in family business. The crowd all moved to the living room to continue enjoying each other's company. Diamond sat on the sofa next to Quenton every so often he would place his hand on her knee, that was exciting her to no end. Then Tasha walked into her grandma's house with an attitude and said to her father "Why you think she gonna be any better than that last woman you had!" Tasha screamed then she walked back out of the door. Quenton jumped up angrily and on his way after her. Diamond stopped him, looked in his eyes and asked if she could go talk to her. Quenton stared deep into her eyes and was powerless; she was so sincere he then nodded his head okay.

When Diamond walked out the door to the porch Sara said,

"That's a good woman that just walked out the door." Quenton sat hoping Tasha didn't start yelling and cursing at Diane like she had done to him so many times before. He only tolerated it because he knew she was hurt, but so was Chantel and so was he. Tasha had wondered to the corner and stood by the light post attempting to light a joint. She jumped when she saw Diamond and quickly put it out. "Can we talk Tasha?" Diamond asked in her most empathetic voice. "What you got to say to me? You just trying to be nice to get next to my daddy!" Tasha yelled. "I do like your father but, it's not about him it's about you. I know you are hurting but-," "Stop! Don't go acting like you know me lady! You don't know what I been through!" Tasha was screaming trying to fight back tears. They were no match for her, they were pouring down her face, she stop trying to restrain them and let them flow freely. "I can't go to school without hearing how somebody seen my crack head mama. It amazes me because we can't see her. She don't even come around to see me or Chantel, but I don't care." Tasha said then wiped the tears from her cheeks. "I don't need her anyway, I don't need nobody, and I damn sure don't need you!" Tasha yelled. Then turned to leave from Diamond's presence. Diamond slid in front of her and looked in her face, "Tasha, stop hurting your self and everyone around you because you're mad. You're not the only one in pain. How do you think your father feels? What about his pain? What about Chantel's pain, you're her older sister you're supposed to be there for her, they both need you." Tasha stopped. Diamond's looked her in the eyes Tasha had never looked at the situation from any other prospective but her own. She never thought about how her father and sister were hurting just like she was. She thought if they felt as bad about it as she did, her father had it really rough because she made it harder for him. This time Tasha felt like an awful person and daughter, she was selfish and mean that wasn't the type of person she wanted to be. Diamond held her and rubbed her back as Tasha cried for her family's pain and the pain she caused, "You get it all out, I got you, I'm here," Diamond soothed. Tasha wiped her eyes and asked Diamond, "How can I get over this anger I have for my mother?" Diamond looked down at Tasha and told her, "Tasha your mother is not what you would like her to be, she has problems like a lot of mothers do." Tears started to well up in Diamond's eyes as she told Tasha about how she was left on a garbage can in some stranger's backyard as a baby. "You know something Tasha? I never knew my parents, but the people that raised me and took care of me are all the parents I need, know, and love. I don't know what type of problems my mother had, but I know God placed me with the right people in my life to look after me. Your daddy and sister are here for you, you be there for them." Tasha was shocked to hear how Diane was abandoned. Tasha wondered how Diane knew it was her mother that left her. "If she didn't do it she let it happen and it's just as bad, but I didn't let it hold me down. It just made me work harder at being worth something. You are a beautiful girl, you can have the world, don't let it slip by. Don't lose your grip on hating and hurting people, start loving, it works and feels better." Diamond let Tasha know if she ever needed to talk she was there for her, she gave her cell phone number and told her to call at anytime. Day or night Diamond was going to be there for her. Tasha hugged her like a daughter would hug her mother. When they went back into the house Tasha ran over to her father hugged him and told him she loved him. Next she was looking for her little sister to do the same to her. Quenton stood shocked, the whole house was shocked. Sara and Felisha had tears running down their faces as Quenton went to hug Diamond. He held her so tight she almost couldn't breathe, and then he walked outside to shed a few tears in private. Diamond felt good, it helped her to finally talk about her own mother.

CHAPTER 10
The Gift

Back at home Josie was Telling Lillie how it was her time to get what she deserved. Lillie sat quietly on the couch as she always did when her mother started to speak. Lillie looked sad as she normally did and watched her mother pace the floor. "My granddaughter is a millionaire. Lillie what you looking like you lost your best friend for? If we work this right we can get everything we every wanted!" Josie yelled. "All I ever wanted was you to be happy mama," Lillie whispered. Josie was taken by Lillie's plea but shook it off. "Well you will have your chance, first I got to put my plan into action, and I know exactly who I need," Josie rambled excitedly. Josie looked like a crazy woman bouncing around laughing to herself. Lillie slowly walked to her room away from the madness. She laid on her bed, buried her head deep into her pillow and cried softly.

"Mr. West there is a call from a Miss. Josie Morgan." Derrick heard his receptionist buzz into his office. "I don't know a Josie Morgan, take a message." Derrick said being irritated as he hated interruptions when he was busy. "Mr. West, Miss. Morgan said it would be in your best interest to get at her." *Get at her? What type of ghetto street talk was that? then-it came to him Josie Morgan was Teresa's sister. He knew he had a good thing with Teresa who was in love with him. He had her wrapped around his finger; he was going to use her to elevate himself to owner and CEO.* Derrick could see in that short encounter with Josie that she was a woman that didn't care who she would hurt to get what she wanted, a quality he happened to possess; he thought he'd hear her out, he had nothing to lose. Derrick picked up the phone, "Hello Josie, this is Derrick, how can I help you?"

"You can help me, but I can help you more!" Josie giggled. Derrick was not interested in getting a piece of ass, he already was getting plenty from Teresa. He tried to rush Josie off the phone. "Look game recognizes game. You trying to work your way up in that company of yours. I can give you a sure shot at it," Josie said. "Look lady are you crazy, I don't have time for this bull shit!" "You better make time. Meet me at the Filmore Hotel." With that Josie hung up the phone. Derrick thought she must be really desperate for some to make lies just to get him. His curiosity got a hold of him and later he was walking into the Filmore Hotel Lobby. It was an upscale place mostly for rich business people. And there she was and even at sixty years she still looked good. If you didn't know her she could be mistaken for a woman of thirty. Derrick took the seat across from Josie. He made it clear that she'd better have a good reason for calling him out of his office in the middle of the day, he was very busy. "Please I know you ain't doing shit but banging my sister. Besides, I know something that will put you higher than her," Josie said. Josie leaned over the table and whispered in Derrick's ear, "I know who Diamond's real mother is," she leaned back over the table and took her seat with a sly devilish smile. Josie continued, "I have full control over her too. Diamond's mother is my daughter Lillie, and I can make her do whatever I'd like." The words slipped off of Josie's tongue like warm honey. Derrick was like a bee lapping up the sweetness. His eyes lit up and a hungry smile crept across his face. "That means Teresa is Diamond's aunt," Derrick said out loud. "Yeah but that don't mean shit, I'm talking about her mama, and I'm Lillie's mama so . . . whatever Lillie gets, I get and more, you feel me?" Josie flashed her perfect set of teeth and winked her eye. At that moment Derrick was reassured that game does recognize game and they were both on the same team. "Okay Miss Lady, so what I got to do for this opportunity?" Derrick flashed his pearly white right back at her. Josie leaned over the table once again; "You see this hotel we are in? I want to get used to this, I want steak, lobster, diamond's houses, cars and a big purse full of money and I know you're gonna help me get it." Derrick wasn't falling for Josie's crap, "That's not all you want." "No, its not, I ain't some young girl. I know what I want and that is a fine man with money and position. If you work with me I can get more of each for you. So for now get us a room so we can finish planning," Josie kissed Derrick on the cheek softly yet seductively. Sitting back in her seat she ran her hands from her neck down her body to her thighs. She could tell she had got his attention and winked at him as she ran her hand up his thigh underneath the table. Derrick read Josie loud and clear. She was not at all discreet. As he walked to the front desk his mind was racing. *I'll play your game lady. I'll do it until I get to the top spot, then I'll dump your ass in the gutter where you came from.*

After a week of vacation Quenton pleaded for Diamond to stay longer. He didn't really have to work hard because she wanted to stay; she was having the best time of her life and falling in love all at once. She was spending most of her time with Quenton and the girls until Felisha told him to share her with the rest of the family. Diamond suggested that the women have a girl's day out including Tasha, Carrie and Chantel. Everyone agreed especially Quenton he was amazed by the change in Tasha. She started helping out around the house, stopped skipping school, staying out late and talking back. Diane had made a real change in her in the short time she was around; Tasha was really bonding with Diane. The girls all went out shopping. Diane bought them all something nice, Felisha tried to argue against it but Diamond insisted. It made her feel good to see those girls happy. Then they all went to get their hair and nails done to match their new clothes. Following that they went out to a really nice restaurant. Diamond, Laura, Felisha and Tasha sat at one booth and Carrie and Chantel sat at the table next to them.

"Miss Diane, would you like to marry my daddy?" Tasha asked. Diamond almost choked on her food. She didn't know what to say. Laura Lee interjected, "I wish I could find me a rich man to marry!" "Laura you got to marry for love not for money, because money is the root of all evil," Felisha said. "No, work is evil, and I can learn to love not working. I can learn to love having money to spend when I want and I can fall deep in love with being able to pay all my bills. I'm tired of bill collectors calling my house looking for money, Talking about rob Peter to pay Paul. Who gave Peter money? He's broke too, Peter, Paul, John and Ringo, they all broke!" every one was cracking up. Although Diamond was laughing in the back of her mind she was thinking, that's exactly why she didn't go boasting about her money. Quenton was so kind; he never let her spend a dime when they went out. She smiled thinking how he was so sweet, and then she thought about how she had to go home. She didn't want to go but she had to but until then she was going to enjoy this time she had. Day's later Quenton took Diamond to his house it was a nice house cleaned up in a way a man and a young girl would do. Diamond visited a few times while she was there but wouldn't stay over night because she wasn't ready. Quenton was, he would kiss her and she would feel like she was exploding inside. She wanted him but after all these years she never had sex always business, then no one worthy enough. Now she wanted Quenton. At the same time she knew this was not the time, Quenton understood this was a lady. The night before Diamond was ready to go home everyone at the house was sad, especially the girls. Chantel asked why mommies always leave and ran upstairs to her room. Tasha hugged Diamond then went to check on her sister. Quenton tried to think of some ways to keep her in California but Diamond told him she had a job and obligations to see about. Quenton couldn't question a working woman and was proud to be with a beautiful, independent, hard working, black woman. Diamond told him she worked for a big company as an associate. He understood about work and business, but he knew his heart was breaking. Diamond spent her last night with him, talking, kissing hugging all night, then she went up the stairs to sleep where the girls slept. She told Chantel she was going to come back that made her feel a little better. Quenton laid in his bed downstairs tortured knowing just up the stairs was his relief he had to get out of bed and take a cold shower. Diamond had to fly back on a public airline because Quenton wanted to drive her to the airport. It would have been too much to explain a private plane. All the way to the airport Quenton tried to think of things to make her stay a little longer. He knew if she loved him, she would come back like she said. They held each other for a long time it wasn't until final boarding before they let each other go. Quenton watched as she took the brief walk down the tunnel to board the plane. It was the longest twenty-eight seconds of his life. Quenton stood there as the stewardess secured the plane door shut. Diamond cried almost the whole trip home.

When Diamond landed Marshal and Teresa was there waiting in her limo to pick her up. Teresa was eager to hear about her new man and tell her about how close she and Derrick had become. Marshal pointed out first thing was first—business then they could giggle and laugh filling each other in on the girl stuff. The ladies agreed. Diamond had to put Diane to rest. Diamond had to come back in full effect. First order of business was the Connors Appliances company. When Diamond got back to the office with Marshal and Teresa they all sat down with Mr. Connors. He was a heavy set, white man with thinning hair and a jolly sense of humor. Between business he would try to crack jokes. He told Diamond about his business and that it was losing money and shares holders were trying to sell off their shares cheap because of the competition. It was hard trying to stay a-float and he didn't know how long he could keep it open. "Then let's offer the people something more. Let's improve the old things and bring in new ones then let's go a broad," Diamond said. Mr. Connors was very impressed with this young woman in the way she did business. Diamond told him first her company would buy up fifty-one percent of the shares. This way they could weed out the shareholders that didn't see growth and start revamping. Connors was nervous about Diamond having so many shares. But he knew it was going to help save the company. He said yes to the plans and that the only stipulation was that he wanted to keep the name of the company the same. He thanked Diamond Corporations for saving the jobs of many of his employees. Diamond mainly had her new extended families jobs on her mind.

"Okay now that we have concluded all of our meetings for the time being. Tell me about your trip and this Quenton-Walker." Teresa quizzed later. Diamond was now smiling Just hearing his name made her heart skip beats. She told Teresa how wonderful he was and about his girls and family. She went into detail when she talked about her long lost best friend Felisha and her new running mate Laura Lee. It felt good to finally have someone to hang with. Diamond told Teresa they all knew her as Diane and not Diamond. None of them knew she was wealthy and none of them knew she was affiliated with Dcorp. Teresa put her hand on

Diamond's shoulder; she could tell Diamond was kind of ashamed that she didn't tell her new friends who she really was. "You say that they are real, you be real. Let them know who you really are, and if they are what you say they are, they won't change-at least not for the worse." Diamond then told Teresa she felt lost being apart from Quenton. "That's love sweet heart," Teresa patted her on the shoulder. "Well, how about you Teresa?" Diamond asked hoping Teresa had realized the snake in Derrick. "Girl I found my soul mate. He's everything I want in a man. I'm glad he came into my life," Teresa beamed. "Well where is he now?" Diamond asked with an artificial excitement.

Laying in a king size bed at the Filmore hotel Josie watched as Derrick rushed to get dressed to run back to his office. This affair had been going on for a little while now and Derrick was starting to question Josie about the plan—Who, what, when, where, and how?

"Don't worry baby, you keep pleasing me and I'll get you that top spot. But it's got to be done right because I know Teresa. She will be the wall we have to get through. But until then you got a few more minutes, get back in bed." Derrick looked at Josie lying there, smiled and started to take off his tie.

"Miss Diane, we're giving daddy a surprise birthday party next month and we would like for you to be there. He's a mess walking around looking sad. He misses you and talks about you everyday, could you please come?" was the message from Tasha left on Diamond's personal 'Diane-line.' Diamond missed Quenton so much they talked on her cell every night for hours she made him laugh when she asked if they could have phone sex. He then asked her about real sex, or making love because that's how he felt about her; he told her he wished he could see her face-to-face to tell her. He wanted to say it so many many times but was afraid he would chase her away. Diamond told him she thinks she started loving him the first time she saw him. Both were silent. Each had put their feelings on the table. Now what's next? As Diamond hung up the phone, she knew one thing was for sure—she was going to that surprise party. Her surprise gift would be something she had saved for a long time—herself. After visiting her parents Beulah and Curtis, Diamond told them about Quenton and his family and how happy she was. Beulah and Curtis had so many times prayed for some good man to come in their daughter's life. She was a success at business but when the day was over she went home to an empty house alone.

Riding back to California on her private plane Diamond heart was beating hard she couldn't wait to see her man. Diamond knew this feeling was love. The surprise party was on a Friday night and she was glad because if things worked out her gift would carry over to the next day. At the Walker house, Tasha had got all the family together then called Quenton to come over. He walked in and saw his parents, brothers, Felisha and his sister Laura Lee. Also there was his cousin Mark and his father Joe—an elderly man who drove the tour bus and often slept in it. He was Ray's older brother. All of the children were their smiling and grinning. The whole family had come over to support Quenton on his big day. Quenton was impressed that Tasha had put this all together for him. He had everything he wanted except one thing. He really wished Diane could have been there. He knew she couldn't come though. Working was a hard thing and a person couldn't just pack up and hop states if they felt like it. Quenton had to make the best of it, besides he had everyone he loved there, all except for her. The party had to go on. Quincy and Laura Lee had music playing everyone was dancing and eating and the whole group got together and danced the electric slide. Tasha started to worry if Diane was coming because it was getting late. Quenton was trying to be convincing of how happy he was, but deep down he wanted to go home and call Diane. When he got to the last gift he said to himself "good, after this I can go home." He looked at the box and he saw it was from Diane. Quenton was so happy his eyes lit up and he was smiling from ear to ear. The whole family all knew that this man was sprung. "How thoughtful of Diane to send a gift," he thought, smiling to himself. He wished that when he opened the box she would jump out. Inside the box was a card with Diane's picture on it and when he opened it, it had her voice saying, if this is not enough, turn around. Quenton turned around and there was Diane standing there. Looking good in a satin dress with a V neckline which revealed a little cleavage, and her hair and nails were done to perfection. Quenton saw her, jumped up and lifted her up. When he brought her down they locked in a passionate kiss. They didn't hear the comments of "get a room," from Laura Lee or Quincy saying, "That's my dog." Quenton looked down at Diane and those sparkling eyes and told her in her ear "I'm so glad you came to my birthday party. This is my best gift." "I've got another gift for you Quenton, me," she replied. "I know baby, I'm glad you're here," he said. Then Diamond whispered in his ear and said, "I mean me," and then gave him a look to let him know she was ready. Quenton's eyes lit up and he said, "You mean?" "Yes," she said, giving him the okay. Quenton excitedly turned around to the family and said a quick "Thank you, but we gotta go," pulling Diamond by the hand toward the door. The family roared in laughter. Quenton yelled "I'll pick you up later girls," and rushed Diamond to the car, overjoyed. He had been waiting for this day for awhile. Diamond thought it was cute how excited he looked, but she knew she was just as excited.

As Quenton was driving he told Diamond that it had been a long time since he had some, so he might be a little rusty. Diamond said "that's okay I wouldn't know the difference because I have never had any." Screech . . . . Diamond's head had involuntarily yanked back as Quenton pulled the car to the side of the street, and then stopped. He parked and looked at her in shock. "What do you mean never had any?" "Just like I said, I've never made love I am a virgin, is that a problem?" she asked. Quenton was shaking his head not knowing what to say, but managed to ask "what have you been waiting for, girl?" Diamond looked up at him with loving eyes and whispered to him, "you." Quenton looked back at her after having one of those heart-grabbing moments and kissed her deeply. As they drove to Quenton's house all he could think of was how this woman chose him to open her door to love. When they got to the house Quenton was nervous, he had never been with a virgin. Mira had plenty of men before him, but Diane was a flower that hadn't been plucked. He began to sweat, Diamond, on the other hand, was ready. She had held out this long waiting for the right man and Quenton was it. So it was on and she had no shame so when they got to the house she took off all of her clothes and laid in bed. Quenton was so hot looking at her naked body, he thought he was going to bust, but he knew that he had to be patient with Diane because this would be her first time. After a lot of foreplay Quenton was trying to get her ready and knowing he couldn't hold it too much longer attempted to enter her. He could see her clinch and the pain in her face and as he moved deeper inside of her he kissed her and talked softly and sweetly to her in an attempt to take her mind off of the pain. It worked and soon after they were making love, resting a bit then going at it again, later they both fell asleep. When Quenton woke up he had Diane in his arms and thought this is the woman that he had waited for all of his life. No way was he going to let her leave him and take all of that good loving. Later Diamond woke up in bed by herself, wondering what happened to that man who had opened the door to her love. What he did to me "whew," she thought, it was magical and she wanted a lot more. Deep in thought she smiled as Quenton walked in with her breakfast or that's what he called it. He had tried but most of the food was burnt and now she knew why they always ate at his parent's house. Diamond ate the burnt food because her man cooked it, and Quenton now relieved of all of that pressure he was storing, and now, was so caught up in trying to please this woman, because she was the one. Quenton had gone and got Diane's clothes to bring to his house, both of them wanted to spend their nights together. Both girls were happy to have a woman around and after a couple of glorious nights it was time for Quenton to go to work. As much as he wanted to stay in bed all morning, he knew that he had a job to do. The plant was having trouble and he had to support his girls and now he thought his soon to be wife. So Diamond watched her man and his two girls get in the car to go to work and the girls to school. She felt like her mother used to feel watching her father and she and her brothers leave in the morning.

Quenton was at work looking at the clock wondering why time was going so slowly, but thinking that when he got home and Diane would be there waiting for him, he was on cloud nine. It didn't even bother him when Ernest like usual tried to talk down to him, no one was going to steal his joy. Later as Quenton and the girls entered the house it was an unfamiliar smell in the house, cooked food. As they looked around the house, it was clean, some things were moved around and Diane was in the kitchen cooking. Quenton looked up and pointed up and said "thank you," because he knew God had brought this woman to him. The girls were looking around happy because their room's was clean. Diamond even washed the clothes. After eating a great meal of roast beef, potatoes and vegetables, everyone left the table full and the girls went to help Diane with the dishes. Quenton went and called his father, Ray. "Hello," Ray said. "Daddy, she can cook!" Quenton yelled. "Well then, the next phone call you make had better be to a Preacher, boy don't let her get away." "She's beautiful, sweet, can cook, clean and she gave me her love. What more can a man ask for" Quenton thought, until he walked into the kitchen and saw Diane and his two girls laughing and washing dishes together. Watching his babies happy and bonding with this wonderful woman made him go to his room and shed a few tears. Quenton was a strong man and after so long trying to get his home together being the daddy, but those girls needed a mama and he had found her.

CHAPTER 11

The Awakening

Teresa was getting worried because it was harder and harder to get in touch with Derrick lately. He always had so much business to take care of "It must be outside business because it sure ain't at this office, he's never here," she said out loud, as she was cleaning up his office and picked up his jacket that was left on the chair. Then she smelled cheap perfume and it was strong and stinky. Teresa was telling herself not to jump to any conclusions. It may have been from an old friend hugging him as a greeting, she hoped, because Derrick was the man she wanted to spend the rest of her life with. He was fine financially well off, smart and in bed he made her sing. "Please Lord don't let this go wrong, I need him" while Teresa was worrying about her relationship Josie was coming into the small house she shared with Lillie who was on the couch watching TV.

Lillie was now a forty-five year-old woman but was so small and shy she didn't look over thirty. After a hard day at the plant she sat there tired and sleepy trying to eat her bowl of noodles that she called dinner. "Lillie, I just got done having me the biggest steak dinner with this fine man that I'm gonna make your daddy!" Josie looked at Lillie as she sat there quietly as usual looking tired and told her. "Don't worry, when I get done you gonna own that plant you working at," and walked in her bedroom singing, leaving Lillie there more scared of what her mother was planning and if it would hurt her daughter Diamond.

Diamond walked around Quenton's small house smiling, thinking this is home to me. I've got to tell Quenton who I am and pray he doesn't get upset or worse, not want me anymore. It was a Saturday morning and when she went to find Quenton, he was at his kitchen table going over papers. Diamond found out he was trying to find out how he was going to get the money to get his parent's restaurant. Quenton now felt that he had a complete family and he really wanted to achieve more for them. Diamond watched and listened as Quenton talked about what he had planned and what he wanted done. Both Quenton and Terry were very smart when it came to business. Terry had the education but Quenton had the know how and drive. Diamond saw that in him and knew if she didn't know him and he came looking for a job, she would hire him on the spot, but being the business woman that she was she couldn't help but put in her two cents. "Quenton if you want the group to be more profitable, you've got to make it a better atmosphere for them." Quenton was listening as Diamond told him what she thought. Initially that the groups were late for shows, when they arrived they had to set up and were grumpy from the long, uncomfortable ride. She suggested that he make it pleasant so that when they got to the shows, they were rested and ready, and what they needed was a new bus which would cost money, but they could make it up by being able to go to more shows. Surely the group wouldn't object because it would pay for itself. Quenton smiled saying "it's sounds good Diane, but it takes money and I have to make sure that I can take care of you and the girls." Diamond was humbled because Quenton had touched her in a way that even he wouldn't believe. Listening to this man tell her he was going to take care of her and he didn't care if she had a dime. Diamond was overcome with emotion and busted out in uncontrollable tears. Quenton went over and hugged her tight and said "baby, you're crying like I asked you to marry me." "Or you?" Diamond asked through her tears and looking him in his eyes. Quenton then got on one knee and said "Diane, would you be my wife?" "Yes, yes, yes!" Diamond cried so loud that the girls came running down the stairs. "What did you do to Miss Diane," Tasha asked, thinking that her father was going to run off the closest thing she had to a mother. Chantel was mad also, looking at her father. "Don't hurt me I just asked Diane to marry me and she said yes," he said. Tasha and Chantel started jumping up and down, yelling, happy that they were going to be a family. Diamond was looking at her new family thinking "my heart made me say yes," but her mind reminded her that they didn't really know who she was but she was not going to ruin this moment and decided to tell them later.

After dropping the girls off at Ray and Sara's house who were overjoyed hearing the news Quenton and Diamond was on their way to the studio where the group was rehearsing when Diamond told Quenton to make a side trip. As they entered the lot to where they sold old and new tour buses Diamond spotted the one she liked right away. Quenton and Diamond got out of the car and after a few moments after watching three white men talking. One of them finally decided to come help. Diamond was upset that they immediately decided they could not afford to buy one of the buses. As they walked around Quenton looked at some of the less expensive tour buses; the cheapest one was fifty thousand dollars. Quenton had a worried look on his face that Diamond did not like to see. The white salesman reluctantly decided to take Quenton around a few blocks, but Diamond could see that he thought it was a waste of time, because he just knew Quenton wasn't going to buy it. Diamond decided to stay and look around. So after they left this young Hispanic fellow named Hector no more than twenty years old saw Diamond and asked her if she needed help. She smiled and said to him, "this is going to be your lucky day." She showed him the bus that she had her eye on and it was the most expensive. The other two salesmen that were standing around started to laugh as Hector showed Diamond inside. It was plush and roomy. But what she was looking for was there. It had a bathroom with a shower, a small kitchen and in the back there was an area with a bed. All of the seats had DVD players, but it was lacking a few other options, which she wanted added. After getting off the bus, Diamond told Hector she was ready to talk business. He was trying to be professional, because this would be a huge commission if he sold this bus. The price was two hundred thousand dollars. Diamond and Hector walked in the office past the two salesmen who didn't know she saw them laughing at the fact of this black woman was thinking she can buy a bus and that one in particular. Diamond made one call to Marshall, who didn't ask questions. He knew it was time for Diamond to start spending some of that money she had stored away in banks. Then Diamond and Hector walked out with the boss hugging the young fellow and put a sold sign on the bus. Diamond walked by the two salesmen and said "who's laughing now," with both of them standing there with their mouths wide open in shock. When Quenton got back and told the man that he would think about buying that bus they test drove, the man said sarcastically "sure you will." Diamond then rushed Quenton to the car telling him he would be late for the rehearsal.

Arriving at the studio Diamond noticed how small it was. The group was all there, Mark, Quincy, and Laura Lee and the band. "You're always the first one here bro, what, is the little woman keeping you at home lately?" Quincy laughed acting like he didn't see Diamond, then turned around and said "oh, hi sis." That sounded so good, how his family was welcoming her into the family. Mark, his cousin, was looking at her like she was interfering or a distraction. He was serious about the group, mainly because he was the lead singer. Diamond knew his kind just like some of the business people she came across. Once they get ahead they go off and leave all the ones that got them there, but it doesn't last. Diamond had the same group she started with and was happy with all of them except Derrick who she didn't trust. That's why she didn't give him big opportunities. He didn't show her that he had what it took. Yes, she thought, both he and Mark are just alike. Laura Lee came over to Diamond admiring her outfit. Diamond had on a white Jean pantsuit. The jeans were tight with a blue stripe on the side, the short jacket had a blue design and she had a low cut blue stretch shirt, she was sharp. As they were talking the group was setting up. Laura told Diamond to come with her next door where they had a place selling barbecue dinners. Laura Lee ordered her dinner, then Diamond was going to get Quenton and herself a dinner when she notice her wallet was missing and thought she must have left it at the dealers. Laura Lee seeing that Diamond didn't have any money said, "girl I got you, I ain't got much but being that you gonna be my sis, whatever I got you can have." Diamond was taken back at how generous this family was.

When they got back with the dinners the fellows were asking where was their food. Laura Lee told Quincy she would save him a bone. "That's why your ass is so big, you're greedy," he said. "And I'm about to be full in a minute, what about you," she replied. Then everyone watched how Diamond took Quenton a dinner with Quenton trying not to act like he wasn't feeling like the man.

"Girl, once you feed them, you ain't gonna never get rid of them," Laura Lee joked. "So that's why you ain't got a man, you're too busy feeding yourself," Quincy laughed. Laura just put a rib in her mouth and smiled at Quincy and said umm, smacking away. The group rehearsed for about an hour with Quenton setting up the sound. Mark, Quincy and Laura Lee was blowing, they were good. Then this older, blond, slim white woman walked into the studio; everyone had a shocked expression. Laura Lee told Diamond that Mark had this old white woman named Jennifer Wilson who Mark brought in to sponsor the group. She was left some money from her late husband and she had a crush on Quenton. And since she was going to spend her money she thought she could run things and get Quenton on top of it. When Jennifer walked in they all had their eyes on Diamond who had no idea who this lady was until she started talking about "who is this?" Seeing how close Diamond was sitting next to Quenton, pointing at her like she was some groupie. Quenton stood up right away and told her "that's my woman," which sounded so good to Diamond. "Well, I don't want her here," Jennifer shouted. Quenton tried to tell her they were trying to practice and that his woman wasn't going anywhere. Jennifer started cussing at Quenton, saying how she wasn't going to spend her money helping out a group that has tramps hanging around. "Oh no she didn't just call me a tramp!" Diamond said to herself, trying to hold back and not show her ass. But when Jennifer called Diamond a bitch that was the last straw. Diamond jumped up and went after her. Jennifer began backing up toward the wall and Quenton was holding Diamond back telling her to calm down. No matter how successful Diamond was she was still a black woman, and you don't call a black woman a bitch unless you're prepared for some drama, and Diamond was going to give it to her, but Quenton was holding her back. Mark was standing in front of Jennifer, Quincy and Laura Lee were in the back yelling "get her Diane," "whoop her ass," Laura Lee was saying, because she knew those were fighting words.

"Look lady, you don't know me. You are not going to come in my face disrespecting my man or me. Do you know I will hurt you." Diamond responded, inside Quenton was happy that this woman was finally getting set straight and excited he had a woman that would stand up for him. "Well, if she stays, I'm leaving," Jennifer yelled. "Then step and don't let the door hit you where the good Lord split you!" Laura Lee yelled back. Jennifer was cussing all the way out the door with Mark following her, trying to get her to stay. When he came back he was saying "now how are we going to get the money to get to our next gig?" Then he looked angrily at Diamond like she had taken the food off of his table. "We'll make it but I won't have any woman thinking they can buy me or disrespecting my woman," Quenton told Mark. After hearing what happened Terry called for a family meeting. "Why can't women come, they're part of the family?" Diamond asked. Quenton thought about it then told Terry "Felisha's got good smarts, but Laura Lee, I know she's out there, but she is a part of the family and I want Diane there. She really has good business sense and she works at a large company as an associate. But most important is that she is going to be my wife."

"Where are you going Lillie," Josie asked seeing Lillie with a bag ready to go out the door. Noticing that it was a bag of clothes Josie began to scream at Lillie. This time Lillie stood there, with her head down and her hand on the doorknob. She knew her mother was planning something that might hurt Diamond and she felt if she left she couldn't use her to do it. "You're leaving me after all I've done for you." Josie was scared now because she knew that Lillie was her only ticket to Diamond and the lifestyle she always dreamed of. She couldn't let her go, so she faked crying, hugging on Lillie and begging her not to go. Lillie fell for it and after she went back to her room, Josie laughed and called Derrick to come get her.

"Are you sure you want me to come?" Diamond asked when Quenton told her about the family meeting. "Of course you're going to be my wife and I want you included in everything I do, what's mine is yours and I want to give you everything you ever wanted." Diamond began to get misty and was attempting to tell him about herself when the doorbell rang and Terry and Felisha were at the door. Then the Walker's showed up with Quincy and

Laura Lee and Joe, and Mark came later. After everyone arrived they were stuffed in Quenton's small dining room to discuss the projects they wanted to do to benefit the family. They had talked about getting a family business for years, and then Quenton got the singing group together. It was a start and usually the men would have a meeting once a month, but it was always the lack of funds that held them back. Most of them had families to take care of except Quincy and Mark; they didn't have jobs other than singing which is why Mark had a problem when they couldn't get to shows. Laura Lee did hair part time and sang part time and she was just getting by. The Walker's were on a fixed income so things were tight, but Diamond loved how they were staying together trying to do things to benefit the whole family.

When the meeting started Terry got edgy when Felisha and his mother started talking about the kids and Laura Lee kept asking what they were going to eat when the meeting was over.

Quenton was trying to keep order while Terry kept giving him an 'I told you so, look.' Diamond was laughing inside at how they were trying to be as professional as possible, but with Laura Lee and Quincy always at it, it was funny to her until Mark said "what are we going to do about the group. We have a gig in Seattle and the bus is broken down and the money we were going to get to fix it is no longer here, because," then he looked at Diamond and continued and said "of a misunderstanding." "The only misunderstanding Mark is that if people don't recognize that I have a woman who I'm going to make my wife and she will not be disrespected, do you understand that," Quenton expressed. Everyone knew this man was serious about this woman and never in Diamond's whole life had someone made her feel so special. "Now that we have that clear we can go to the first business at hand. I found a building in a nice spot in the city to open up the restaurant. The owner said he would try to hold it for us, but we have until the end of the month to come up with at least fifty thousand dollars, just to hold it. I called the bank and they rudely said no, so we will need extra income to get the business started," Terry said. Everyone got quiet until Quenton said "well, I'm going to take a second mortgage if it's okay with my fiancée, to get the bus fixed. We did look at new ones but we need to get rolling for our next gig." Then he looked at Diamond waiting for her to say yes. "No," Diamond said. She couldn't stand the thought of Quenton taking a second mortgage on his house, even though it was a very unselfish thought, but her response left the family wondering why she wouldn't let Quenton help the family. Mark mumbled something under his breath. Diamond took a breath and asked if she could see if she could find some investors to come up with the funds. "Oh yeah, right, if the banks ain't gonna loan us no money, where we going to find somebody who would," Mark said looking at Diamond like she was crazy. Diamond excused herself and left the room.

Some of the family felt Mark had embarrassed her to leave as Quenton angrily looked at Mark. Minutes later Diamond walked back in the room and told Terry to call the bank. "What are you talking about?" Terry asked. "Just call," Diamond insisted, while the family sat around arguing, Terry was on the phone. Quenton observed a shocked look on Terry's face, who then looked over at Diamond. He then hung up the phone and went to the computer and looked up an account in the name of the Walker Family Fund. Felisha then watched her husband looking so strange that she asked "what's wrong Terry?" "Nothing is wrong," then he looked at Diamond again and asked "lady, who do you know?" Now all of the family was wondering what was going on. Terry took a breath then told the family that he just finished talking to the bank manager and he said they now have a family account with two hundred-fifty thousand dollars in it and that if they needed anything else, just to call. He added that the bank was supposed to be very nice to them. "What, Terry you're lying!" Laura Lee yelled. "Look at the computer, it shows the account. How did you do it Diane, and who do we have to pay back. What are the terms?" Now the whole family was on the edge of their seats wondering if this was really true as all eyes were on Diamond. "There is no interest, no fees, it's an investment," Diamond said. "But from who?" Quenton asked, confused. "It's from me," Diamond said, realizing this was the time to come clean. She couldn't let her new family, who was willing to share everything with her, to worry about another dime. "Sis, you got it like that?" Quincy asked. "Diane what do you do at that company you work at, what's the name?" Quenton asked. "It's the Diamond Corporation," Diamond said. "Wait, wait!" Felisha yelled, "That's your name Diamond!" Everyone appeared to be in shock, waiting for Diamond to say something. Then Quenton asked again "what do you do there?" Diamond did not look at him, but felt the heat on her neck as she nonchalantly said, "I work there, I manage it, I . . . own it I'm Diamond." There was complete silence, and then Terry jumped up excitedly. "You're that Diamond, you're the one that bought all of those shares and pulled our company out of the hole?" Diamond nodded, yes. All of the family was staring at each other with their mouths open in shock. Terry then stated "That's not all you own. I read up on your corporation. Is it true that you own over twenty companies, shares, and even a fashion design label." "Those are your clothes in our store. I should have known, but why didn't you tell us?" Felisha asked. "Yes, why didn't you tell us Diamond, that is your name," Quenton said and walked out of the room. Diamond put her head down and said "I guess he don't want to marry me now," then she got up to follow him out. "Hell, I'll marry you!" Quincy yelled at her as she walked out, leaving the family in shock.

When Diamond walked into Quenton's bedroom, he was sitting there on the bed, looking at the floor and shaking his head. She sat down next to him and took his head in her hands and turned it toward her to look into his eyes. "Quenton, I'm sorry I didn't tell you who I really was, but you've got to understand how hard it is to be able to socialize with people when they know you own companies and have money. Because then they treat you as if you're not real, and it's hard for me to see who really wants to know me. I wanted to tell you so many times, but I was afraid you would change and now look how you're acting. I am a very successful business woman, who loves you with all of my heart," Diamond was looking at Quenton hoping that he understood. Quenton thought to himself what can I give this woman, she must have everything. Why did she choose me, she must have had lots of rich successful men trying to get at her, but her eyes told him that she loved him. And it wasn't like she had a husband and kids, she just hid that she was a very rich, powerful woman who he was in love with. "So now what am I supposed to do with you D I A M O N D?" Diamond smiled and said "just love me. Now come on we've got a house full of family." Quenton took her in his arms wondering how he was going to come to terms with this. "Hey sis, let me holler at you," Quincy said as they came back in the room. "No, don't make me holler at you!" Quenton said. "I know what you want Q and I'm letting everyone know that Diane . . . Diamond will not be giving, or loaning any money. You weren't asking for money before." "That's because we didn't know she had any," Laura Lee laughed. "Well, I'd like to know how rich are you Diamond, are you a millionairist?" Quincy asked. "You can say that," Diamond told him. "I know what I can say I want to know what you say." "Yes, I do have a few million." "How many million," Laura Lee asked. "A few hundred million," Diamond responded. Before she could finish Laura was jumping up and down like she was in church. Quincy was slapping five with everyone and yelled, "Quenton, you done hit the jackpot you lucky motherfu . . ." he then stopped when his mother gave him a dirty look. The whole family was excited about Diamond and the money she deposited and how to spend it. When Tasha came in the room and said there are two men at the door. "Oh, that must be my next surprise," Diamond said. She figured if she was coming out she might as well go all of the way and told the dealer to drop off the new tour bus. When the family came outside everyone was ecstatic with the huge black bus with a gold stripe. It had all of the features in it including bathroom and shower, a kitchen, DVD players at each seat, but Diamond had the dealer add a system set up for CD's and intercoms at each seat. She also had one placed in the back room so Joe the bus driver could talk to each individual without having someone having to get up or disturb others. It also had shades that were put in between the seats that you could pull down. This would allow people to read, sleep or whatever, without someone watching them. That was one of Diamond's ideas. She also had them add a sensor that was put around the bus, so that if they were stopped at night and anyone came close to the bus, it would set off an alarm. And the last was a seat sensor that could read the driver's body movement so that if his body started to go to sleep, it would send a small jolt to wake up the driver. Everyone liked that idea even the dealer who wanted to order some for his other buses. Joe was taken back when Diamond told the dealer to give a set of keys to him. Mark was now looking shamed that he underestimated this sister and to think that he was upset that Jennifer was kicked out, not knowing this woman probably had more money in her change purse than Jennifer had all together. After looking at the bus the whole family went back in the house all happy and excited. The dealer then gave Quenton the papers to sign. Quenton asked about the payment arrangements, which made the man look at Diamond in confusion. "It's already paid for in the name of Quenton Walker." Quenton looked at Diamond. She smiled and said "it's that other birthday gift for you" and gave him a wink. Quenton shook his head, signed the papers and took the other set of keys. Laura Lee looked at felisha and said, "I think our first family meeting with us woman went off very good, don't you think?" "They should have asked us a long time ago," Felisha said now looking at the men.

CHAPTER 12

The Pre No!

The next few days were difficult with people calling asking for money. Old cousins and people Quenton had not talked to in years, and after he told the family to keep quiet he was suddenly getting all of these calls. Now he knew what Diamond was talking about. People that were thinking he had money because he was with Diamond began acting differently and treating him like he was their best friend in the world. As Diamond and Quenton laid in bed, Quenton said, "Baby I bet you had to live your life in a fish bowl, not being able to get out without all of these vultures after you. I don't blame you a bit now for not telling people, but I would like to know why you bought shares in Conners." "At first it was just business, then it was personal and your company has potential, it just needs a lift." Quenton then told her about the company banquets he stopped going to. Because at first he didn't have anyone to go with and second because of Ernest, his boss and ex best friend, and how he did him. Diamond told him "You can look at that situation two ways. One is that he stabbed you in the back and was a false friend, or on the other hand you could look at the fact that if he didn't cheat with Mira, that you might have still been in that old situation, instead of laying next to me." Quenton looked at his woman and told her that she has such a way at looking at things, she must have been brought up right.

Meanwhile Curtis noticed lately at the plant how sad Lillie was looking lately. She rarely smiled, but she seemed happy working when she first started. And she uses to sit down and have lunch with him, but now she would just sit in the corner by herself getting thinner and thinner. And her eyes, if you could see them, they were red like she had been crying all night. "Are you okay Lillie?" Curtis asked. Lillie was scared now more than ever. She had overheard Josie her mother talking on the phone about how she was going to get paid and live in a big house with a fine man and finally get what she deserved. She didn't mention taking Lillie into this world, which Lillie at this time didn't care, about herself. She worried what Josie planned to do with her daughter. When

Curtis asked her what was wrong, she wanted to tell him and beg him to help her. But she was so scared of Josie that she might even hurt him that she just walked away leaving Curtis wondering who had hurt this woman.

The day of the banquet for the Conner's Plant, Diamond had outfits flown in from her store. Never before seen dresses for Felisha and herself. Felisha had on a long silver beaded dress and Diamond had on a long black silk dress, which was sleeveless and split down the back, and it fit like a glove. They both had gone to an exclusive salon to get their makeup applied and Laura Lee did their hair. They looked good. Terry and Quenton were beaming from ear to ear at their women all made up with fancy hairdo's. They had on sharp tuxedos as a request from Diamond. When they stepped outside there was a long white limo waiting to take them to the banquet. Terry and Felisha were really getting into this lifestyle. Quenton was thinking that back home where Diamond lived; this was how she rolled. And he was thinking that she lived in a modest house, and she did only it was the guesthouse next to her mansion. When they arrived at the luxury banquet room the ladies walked in first with Quenton and Terry following behind watching as both of these fine sisters swished those big hips as they went in the door. Quenton and Terry looked and smiled at each other and gave each other a pound. They knew that their women would be some neck turners. Diamond looked around and noticed there were about two hundred people there. All of the workers were shocked to see Quenton come in since he had stopped attending these events after Ernest backstabbed him.

Ernest was sitting up front with his date, a white blonde who looked about twenty years old with fake boobs sticking out. Ernest watched when the couples came in and was staring Diamond down wondering who this woman was. Quenton, trying to move on after what Ernest did, didn't like the way Ernest was eye balling his woman. Terry always-hated Ernest for what he did to his brother and how he tried to ruin his life by breaking up his marriage, but he still had to work with him. Terry leaned over to his brother and whispered "Don't worry he got the dirty rock, while you got the Diamond." Quenton gave his brother a shoulder hug and the couples sat down. Diamond was told by Terry that Mr. Conners stopped coming to the banquets since he moved away to live in Florida, so she didn't have to worry about being recognized and could just sit and have a nice time with Quenton and Terry and Felisha. The banquet began and people were talking and eating. Quenton kept telling Diamond how proud he was and how special he felt sitting with her and how beautiful she looked. Diamond felt good that it wasn't about status it was about her just being a woman, being with her man. At the head table was what Terry said was for the big shots. His boss, Mr. Richards, a middle aged white man was there along with a few other associates. Diamond liked being on Quenton's arm and letting everyone see that he had moved on from what Ernest did to him. Mr. Richards then got up to talk and told everyone that they had a special guest and out of the back rooms Mr. Conners came walking in. Everyone stood up and gave him a standing ovation. Terry and Quenton were both excited to see Mr. Conners, because he didn't come around to the plant much and when he did, he only stayed a short time talking mostly with the heads. Sometimes Mr. Richards didn't get to see him, so they were impressed. Diamond looked at some of these men's faces, and their behavior was as if they were looking at the President of the United States. After everyone sat down Mr. Conners started telling the people how the company was in trouble at one time, but was looking to stay open and go higher, which had all of the people clapping again. Quenton and Terry knew why the company pulled through and it was because of this beautiful sister sitting at their table. Quenton was unsure how to deal with being with this woman who had achieved more than he ever could or ever thought of, and she was lying in his bed at night.

Diamond listened and was hoping that Mr. Conners wouldn't recognize her, but as he talked and looked around, then he saw her face. He then stopped talking, just staring at her. People were wondering what was wrong with him. Diamond thought "oh no, he sees me, please don't say anything." "Diamond, is that you?" he asked. Diamond knew she had been spotted and gave him a nod and a weak wave. "I can't believe it, what are you doing here and why aren't you sitting up here?" Mr. Richard appeared stunned because he didn't know what Mr. Conners was talking about. "Ladies and gentlemen I want you all to meet Diamond Bradford of the Diamond Corporation." Now all of the big heads knew of the Diamond Corp. and were moving around to see her, while in the back of their minds they were hoping they could get close to her. Mr. Conners went on to say how "this young lady saved this company by coming to our aid." Ernest was straining his neck in shock and wishing now that he and Quenton were still friends, so he could get next to this powerful lady. "What are you doing here at our little gathering?" Mr. Conners asked. Diamond thinking how Quenton was feeling kept it short and sweet. "I'm just here with my man," and all of the sisters laughed. She then looked at Quenton who didn't really know how to feel with all eyes on him, and probably wondering how he could get such a successful woman. Terry was thrilled with all of the attention on them. For once he had all of the bosses watching him and Quenton. Mr. Conners tried to get Diamond to come up front, but she declined and remained with her fellow and family. He again thanked Diamond for the rescue and talked a few minutes more, then ended his speech and told everyone to enjoy the rest of the evening. He then walked over to Diamond with all eyes on him and with all of his associates following behind, and pulled up a chair to sit with the family. Quenton and Terry were shocked to no end having never had a conversation with Mr. Conners in all the years working at his plant, and now here he is at their table. Quenton noticed how Diamond was so confident and didn't appear to be impressed. She wasn't, because she was use to talking to a lot of important business people with even more status than Conners. "Diamond I'm so glad you're here, I've been trying to call you and all I get is you're on vacation," he said. Diamond sat back, relaxed, and told Conners "I am here with my fellow, Quenton Walker, and his brother Terry and his wife Felisha. Both Quenton and Terry work at your company." "Oh, I know them, I just never got to speak with them," he said. "Why not, they are both very dedicated and committed to your company?" Diamond asked. Quenton and Terry were both looking back and forth at each other while this sister was building them up. "Well then

I think that I need to talk to them and you too, can we have a meeting on Monday? I'm supposed to go home, but I'll stay over. I really need to talk shop with you and you're a hard lady to get in touch with," he begged. "Fred, I'm sorry, but I'm leaving to go back home on Sunday as I have other business issues that I have to get to," she told him. Fred, she's on a first name basis, was what was going on in most of the men's minds that huddled around the table. Even they couldn't call him that. "How can I get you to stay, maybe Quenton is the answer. Can he get you to stay a few more days," Mr. Conners asked. He was hoping so and looked at Quenton who was beaming with pride. He knew that this was his moment. "Diamond, won't you stay a few more days for me?" he asked, but in his mind he never wanted her to leave although he knew who she was and what she did. Diamond was a very important lady and just couldn't run away from all of her obligations, but he was hoping she wouldn't shame him in front of all of these people and say no. "Anything for you Quenton," was what she said. "That's my girl" he thought to himself. So the meeting was set and while Terry and Quenton and the gentlemen sat there talking business, for them it was the opportunity of a lifetime. Diamond was glad to see these brothers shine, they had been looked over for too long and had many ideas to improve the plant, and now they were getting their time. Conners was amazed at these men and asked Mr. Richards why was he hiding these talented men. He continued to say that if they had more control maybe the company would have never been in trouble. Quenton was feeling so proud and Terry was looking at his boss with a smile of importance. Diamond knew the feeling and wanted to let them have their moment, and decided to go outside with Felisha to get some air. When they got outside Diamond noticed Felisha getting misty. "What's up girl?" she asked. "Diamond, what you did for those two brothers is so wonderful and my Terry, I haven't seen him this happy in so long," she then hugged her. Diamond told her that she loved all of them and "that's what families do." "Girl, I've got to go fix my face, these tears are messing up my makeup," Felisha laughed and left to fix herself up. As Diamond stood outside looking at the stars, thinking of Quenton and being married, she wondered how they were going to do it. Would he come and move with her, or would she move in with him. She knew they had to talk about it eventually someone was going to have to make that move. Then all of a sudden she heard a voice say, "Hello Diamond, I'm Ernest," and he put his hand out to shake Diamond's hand, but she didn't give it. She gave him a small nod, knowing about him. Ernest went on trying to say how proud he was of her. Being a beautiful, black, successful sister and how he would love to work more with her and that he wasn't married to Conners Appliances and if he had the opportunity, he could really be an asset at Diamond Corporation. Diamond listened to all of that crap and when Quenton walked out he immediately became angry because he saw Ernest trying to make a move on his woman. But he was not going to let Ernest ruin this for him and he decided to see how his woman was going to handle this. "Oh, hello Quenton, I see you're doing well having this beautiful lady to finally open doors for you. You must be very happy," Ernest stated. Quenton was steaming inside as Ernest was trying to make him seem that he wasn't capable of achieving anything without help. Diamond saw a look from Quenton that she had never seen before, said to Ernest "look, I didn't get this far in life by being phony, so I'm going to get real with you Ernest. You can't come to me like that because I know your kind. I see you often in this business. You're untrustworthy, disloyal and as fake as your girlfriend's boobs, so spare me all that crap you're dishing out, because I'm not Mira." "Whew, did my woman just make it very clear to you that your presence is not needed here," Quenton interjected. Needless to say Ernest was embarrassed, knowing that if he had not dogged out Quenton he would have had the opportunity of a life time, to be associated with one of the biggest company's out there. That made Conners appliances look like a small corner restaurant, Ernest had to turn around and walk out. Quenton, looking down at his woman and said, "Baby for so long I wanted to tell him off, but it's not about him anymore because like you said, he did me a favor. If it wasn't for him I probably would have still been stuck in hell. I can't believe this night Diamond, you surprised me of the huge amount of respect that people show you, but they don't even know how loving and kind you are. What you did for me and Terry tonight was so special, thank you." He then pulled her close to him and hugged her and kissed her, then they just stood out there under the stars holding each other. On the ride back home Terry told Diamond that she had made his night.

Meanwhile back at home, later that night while Teresa and Derrick were in bed sleeping at his house, his phone rang. It was three in the morning and Teresa acted like she was asleep when Derrick looked at her to make sure she was he then took the phone in the bathroom. "I told you not to call me on my home phone and do you know what time it is? No, I can't come now; she's here with me asleep. I can't come, NO." Teresa overheard Derrick talking and finally knew the truth. Teresa had suspected but she tried to convince herself it wasn't true because she didn't want to believe her man was cheating on her. After Derrick hung up and got back in bed, he leaned over and thought Teresa was still sleeping, laid down and thought to himself that he might have to come up with his own plan. He couldn't keep waiting on Josie, who was wearing him out and knowing that Teresa would find out some day, but after he got the top spot in Diamond Corp. he was going to drop both of them, being that he didn't care about either one.

After the banquet things got crazy with people acting strange knowing who Diamond was. Chantel didn't know the difference, but Tasha was upset that Quenton wouldn't let Diamond buy her a car. And at the family house more family were coming over to ask for favors and getting upset with Quenton because he wouldn't allow Diamond to give out any money and he wasn't going to have people bothering his woman. Some of the family and friends would call Quenton stingy or worse, Mr. Diamond that really set him off. Diamond again told Quenton that was why she kept her life a secret, how even he was acting different. She was still his Diane, but she was also Diamond and it was hard for him to keep them separate. Terry and Quenton were nervous all weekend about the meeting on Monday, knowing that all of the heads would be there. When Monday came around Quenton was up at five in the morning, at his desk going over what he wanted to say. Diamond woke up and got out of bed and put her arms around his neck and told him not to worry about the meeting, it was going to be okay and that she had a way to relieve his nervousness. Quenton asked what was it, Diamond smiled and took him by the hand and led him to the bedroom.

Later she was suited up in her professional gear; a black pinstripe skirt suit with black pumps with the high heels and her hair was fashioned in a simple, yet elegant style, which enhanced her facial features. Diamond, Quenton and Terry walked through the plant to the conference room. All eyes were on her and she could hear the sisters say, "you go girl," proud of this young black woman. When the three of them entered the room it was full of executives all waiting for Diamond. Ernest was there in the back wishing he was Quenton right now. Mr. Richards had a seat for Diamond up front with Mr. Conners and had seats for Quenton and Terry toward the middle, so they could be close to her. Diamond wasted no time letting everyone know that Quenton and Terry were to be seated up front next to her, so she had Conners on one side, Quenton and Terry on the other side. They were overwhelmed at the power she possessed and after listening to Mr. Conners talk about what he wanted to do with the company, his plans for the future and the new opportunities, it was Diamond's turn. Diamond did what she did best; she took over that boardroom. She talked about profit, value, and long term goals, expansion all of the things she was going to have done. Everyone listened as this young black woman showed why she was so successful. She was a very smart and intelligent businesswoman. Quenton and Terry just kept looking back and forth at each other in amazement; both of them so proud of her taking on the big heads and having them listening to every word that came out of her mouth. After the meeting Mr. Conners, Richards, Quenton, Terry, Diamond and Ernest stayed behind. Diamond told Conners that she would feel better if Quenton would have a better position at the company, because he could look after her interest in the company. Conners wanted to give Quenton Richards's job. Richards was turning red and sweating, and then they decided to give him Ernest's job and move Ernest down to Quenton's job. Conners was not aware of the drama between these two and told Ernest it was just business, not personal. Diamond thanked him then offered Conners the use of her private plane to use to go home, since he changed his flight for the meeting. "Private plane, my woman's got a plane," Quenton said to himself. His mind was starting to overload with all of these events. It was getting to be too much and when they were leaving out of the door, Ernest walked over to Quenton and he was extremely mad. He made sure that no one heard him and said "So big man how does, it feel to have to sleep with the boss to get ahead, must make you feel pretty cheap!" "Not as cheap as going behind my best friend's back and screwing his wife!" Quenton shot back but deep in his mind he was feeling like people thought he couldn't stand without Diamond's status.

After a couple of days Diamond decided to ride back with the group on their new bus to their show in Seattle, then everyone would come back in stay a few days at her home. The ride was romantic for Quenton and Diamond. They talked about everything and Quenton was forgetting about Diamond and seeing Diane. Everyone came, Laura Lee, Quincy, Mark, the band, Tasha and Chantel came along with Felisha, Terry and their kids, while Joe drove the bus. Everyone talked about how wonderful the bus was and the group did a great job at the show. When they got there, they were well rested and the women had the kitchen always filled with cooked food. They had a bathroom and a shower, so they didn't have to keep stopping. Joe was thrilled with the bus and Quenton let him keep it at his parent's home where there was more parking space. Joe kept going between Mark's and the Walker's homes. Now he was living in the bus, which was okay with Quenton. Halfway to Diamond's home she sat up front and told Terry and Quenton that she needed their help. Both of the men knew they couldn't and wouldn't say no to her after all she had done for them. Diamond told them that she had a plant in New York and that it wasn't doing well. She further stated that she had received a letter from an employee there stating there were a lot of problems there and that she should care more about her employees than the money she was making. Both Quenton and Terry both knew whoever this was didn't know Diamond, but it was bothering her. Diamond decided that after she had finished catching up on her business at home, she was going to fly up there as Diane and find out what was going on. But she needed Terry and Quenton to go over the management side to determine how the situation could be straightened out. Quincy, overhearing the conversation, convinced them that he should come down and help Diamond on the floor by pretending to be her brother, so he could watch out for Diamond. Quenton thought that was a good idea, but knew deep down that Quincy also wanted a vacation. When the bus arrived at Diamond's mansion everyone was in awe at the size of the place. The kids ran off the bus, Quincy looked at Quenton and said "You lucky mother fu—," then stopped when Chantel ran back and asked her father if they could live here. When everyone got off the bus they were shocked trying to take in the mansion Diamond lived in. Then Jose and Maria, her helpers, and their two children Maurie and Edmond came out to greet Diamond. Jose told her they were glad that she was back and had everything in order for her. "Girl you got a maid and a butler?" Laura Lee asked. "Yes, and they cook too," Diamond added. "Well I ain't going home," Laura laughed. Diamond gave the group the guided tour around the place. She showed them the guesthouse then took them into the mansion where all she could hear was oohs and ahhs as they walked to the basement area. The guys were excited at the kick it area, and couldn't wait to get to the bar. Then Diamond opened the door to the outside where the pool and tennis court was. They were quite impressed but what really took them to the top were her cars, the theater and the studio that Diamond had built. It was bigger than the one they used back home and had all of the new features. They were like school kids getting so into it. She had a wide variety of equipment and there was a weight room next to that which was professionally equipped. Quincy whispered to Quenton, "your woman got all this, if I was you and she was my woman she would be popping out my second baby by now." Quenton was overwhelmed like everyone else at all of the material things Diamond possessed, but he loved her for her and he couldn't understand why people couldn't see it. It was starting to bother him that he felt people might think of him as a kept man. He worked hard for what he got in order to provide for his girls and himself. Even his kids were not satisfied now. After the tour everyone had to pick out their rooms. Laura Leeand Tasha chose the upstairs and the fellows picked the basement. Terry, Felisha and the kids were going to stay in the guesthouse. After everyone got squared away, Quenton told the group he wanted to meet up with everyone in an hour, until Diamond gave him an elbow to his ribs, "let's make that two hours," he smiled knowing that his woman was ready for him. Diamond led Quenton to her big bedroom that was like a show place with candles and flowers. The decorations were in light gold colors and it was beautiful, but she rarely slept in it and she wasn't about to sleep in it now. When they got in the room they both rushed to pull off their clothes. All through the long ride the tension was up. Quenton was so hot that he wanted to take her in the backroom of the bus, but it was too many noisy people. But now it was just them and that beautiful bed. They made love for hours not looking at the clock. By the time they got to the meeting in the basement, four hours had passed by. When they entered the basement everyone was there. Laura Lee was bartending, and some of the band members were watching TV. Mark, Quincy, Terry and Joe were playing poker. "Damn man is it that good, you ain't never been this late to a meeting," Quincy laughed. Quenton tried not to smile but his grin let people know that his woman was very good at pleasing him. "Pull up a chair Quenton, because we know you got some money," Quincy joked. "I'm just gonna break you all and send you home broke," Quenton replied. He was beginning to relax from the stress of all the things going on. The ladies talked outside the basement and were on the patio drinking margaritas, while the fellows were getting loud and enjoying themselves. Diamond excused herself and decided to go upstairs and catch up on things and while she was going over some bills she felt someone standing behind her. It was Mark and he was so close she could feel his body heat on hers. Diamond moved away looking strangely at him. He considered himself a ladies man and felt that he could get any woman he wanted. Mark was fine looking and a singer and had never been turned down. As he tried to look at Diamond with what he thought was a sexy glance, it did nothing but set her off. "Look Mark, when you first met me and I ran your friend Jennifer off, you was extremely rude and disrespectful to me. Now you want to rub up on me. Well, let me tell you something, I don't appreciate it. You know I'm Quenton's woman and just this once I'm going to let you off the hook and not tell him, but don't ever try that shit again, because I will tell him if it happens again. Do you understand?" Mark was shocked. He had waited a long time after finding out who she was to get her alone in order to make his move and she shot him down. Ashamed, he walked back downstairs hoping no one would notice, but game recognized game. When he sat down both Quincy and Terry gave him a look that told him if he tried to hurt their brother that he would have to deal with both of them. The poker game went on until two in the morning, and then the three brothers went to the studio and sat down to talk. "Quenton you need to keep your eyes open when it comes to your woman. Diamond is no ordinary woman and men are going to try to get at her. Some she might not be able to get off of her," Terry said. Quenton wondered what Terry was talking about when Quincy said "You ought to know more than us about how you can't trust your friends, and sometimes you even have to watch your family, you feel me?" Quenton knew now that they must have been talking about Mark and decided that instead of kicking his ass with his woman and kids there, he would wait until they got back home to deal with him. Quenton left the studio and walked around the whole place looking at all of the rooms, checking out her cars, and then he went to the bedroom. Diamond was sleeping soundly and he got in bed laying there beside her, wondering how he could be so blessed to find a woman he loved so much, but still not knowing how to deal with the facts of their situation. Most people would think that if you married a rich person it was always because of the money. Then he thought of something that was going to make everything right. Much happier now, he went to sleep.

The next morning everyone got together for a barbecue. Curtis and Beulah came over and Dennis arrived with his family. Then Teresa and Marshal showed up, all eager to meet Diamond's man and his family. Everyone was getting along fine and Beulah was getting a kick out of Laura Lee and Felisha. Dennis struck up a conversation with Terry and Quincy while Curtis took Quenton aside to talk to him about his daughter. "Diamond is a good woman as you know and all we want is her happiness. Now I'm hoping you can do this and protect her because sometimes she can't see the people who are not there for her, but there for what she can do for them." Quenton assured Curtis that he was going to take care of Diamond and let the world know that he was real. "Teresa, why are you so quiet and where is Derrick?" Diamond asked. Teresa had cried all of her tears out and now she was just numb, told Diamond that Derrick was cheating on her and was probably with his other woman right now. "Are you sure Teresa?" Diamond asked. Teresa gave Diamond a look like she knew. "But I'm not giving up, I love that man and I'm going to fight to keep him," she said and then told Diamond that she would see her later, then she left. Time went on and Curtis and Beulah, Dennis and his family were now leaving. Curtis made sure that Diamond promised that she would attend the company picnic Dennis set up for the family of the worker's to get together and meet each other. After they left Diamond called Marshal and Quenton and Terry into her office to talk business. They talked about the trip to New York and what they had to do. Marshal took the floor and with Diamond's permission let Quenton and Terry know all the assets and financial reports on Diamond Corporation when he finished reading off all of the various companies, investments and fashion designs. Terry started to choke and Quenton was shaking his head in shock. "The reason I'm telling you all of this Quenton is because I want you and Terry to come help me run all of this. And Quenton, like you said, what's mine is yours." Diamond explained. Now all eyes were on Quenton who when he said that he didn't know she had assets of three hundred million dollars. That would sound funny, him throwing in his meager assets with hers, and what would people think of him, just stepping into a fortune. But he had a way to fix it so it was time to do it. "Diamond you know that I love you and when we get married I want everyone to know it's for you and not your money, so I'm gonna have Terry draw up a prenuptial agreement. If by chance our marriage somehow didn't make it, I wouldn't be entitled to any of your money." Quenton said then began to smile thinking that he had done a good deed. Diamond felt like someone had stabbed her in the heart, asked Quenton "why would you think that I needed to be assured that you were not marrying me for money. I know that and I love you.

And my marriage is not going to fail and I don't want that holding over my head." Tears were streaming down her face. Quenton was tearing up inside watching his woman cry. He was confused and he told her that he thought he was doing the right thing. Then she told him "right for who not for me. This prenupt is because people made you feel insignificant. That's what they wanted, please don't let people dictate our life Quenton," Diamond cried. It was hurting Quenton seeing his woman all broken up, but he had to let her and everyone else know that he was a man that could make decisions and stand by them. He felt that the prenup was necessary for him to ensure that everyone, including Diamond, knew how sincere he was. Only Diamond didn't see it that way. Quenton felt that he knew what was coming next, but he had to be a man and he didn't want to start their life bowing down even to the woman he loves. With tears in her eyes Diamond said "I'm not signing a prenup and the only paper that I'm signing is a marriage license and if that's not enough," Diamond stopped and finished with "then I guess it's no marriage," and she walked out. Quenton felt his heart drop as he watched his woman walk out of the room. Both Marshal and Terry told Quenton they understood what he was trying to do. Marshal thought it was very admirable and always hoped that one day Diamond would find a good man, and she did. But now she was thinking like a woman and not the businesswoman. She could not understand what this man was trying to do and it hurt him to see her so hurt. They had grown very close working together, and she was like a daughter to him. He told Quenton that he hoped things would work out between him and Diamond, because he felt he was the man for her, and then he left. Quenton was still in shock and just stood there staring in space wondering what had just happened. "Did I just lose the best woman that I ever had, did that really happen?" he thought to his self. He felt like she walked out of the room carrying his heart with her. Terry was sticking by his brother's side feeling his pain. He understood but didn't like the idea of the prenup and tried to talk Quenton out of it. He didn't need to make Diamond even feel like there might be problems with their marriage. He could see by the way she looked at Quenton, that when she said I do. She means it. But Quenton made her see something else, possible failure. Quenton went to the bedroom and found out Diamond had moved over to the guesthouse to sleep, along with Laura Lee and Tasha. Terry decided to stay at the mansion knowing the guesthouse was probably off limits to all men about now. "I can't believe Quenton would let people dictate our future," Diamond cried. All of the women just listened as Diamond cried out in pain. "I thought he loved me!" "Now girl, you know he loves you, he is just feeling insecure," Felisha said. "Yeah, with all of the things you have, it probably has him confused. My brother is used to working hard for things and striving to achieve. How can he go higher than all of this," Laura Lee said. Diamond looked at her and said "by being my husband and having a family." All of the women were shedding tears knowing and feeling Diamond's pain and knowing that Quenton was feeling the same way. Quenton laid in the bed hoping that Diamond would come in and part of him wished he could take back what had happened, the other part told him he did the right thing. The next day Diamond said her good byes to Terry, Felisha, Quincy and Laura Lee and all of the kids, who did not know what had happened. When they got on the bus to leave, Quenton waited to see if Diamond would at least say goodbye, because he really wanted to see her. But after awhile when she didn't come he got on the bus and they pulled off, leaving Quenton's heart behind.

"Look at him, just pitiful, pit-i-ful, sitting up there by himself looking like a lost puppy dog," Quincy said not letting up on Quenton. "Man you let that woman get away, you must be plain crazy. That woman has the three B's," Quincy said. "What's the three B's?" Terry asked sitting next to him. "Beauty, booty and bank, what else can you ask for and he loves her. He's crazy," "He has his pride," Terry said trying to help Quenton out. "Pride hell, what's pride going to do for him when his Johnson wakes him up in the morning and all he got is the five sisters." "Five sisters, what's that?" Terry asked. Quincy then held his hand out and started pointing at each finger, "five sisters." "Leave him along Q you see he's hurting," Laura said, watching as Quenton stared out the window thinking how he could replay that day. He heard his brother talking and as much as he hated to admit it, Quincy was right. His pride made him feel like he had to prove to people that he wasn't going to be a kept man. But when he woke up the other morning, it was Diamond that was in his arms and the more he thought about her and how he lost her was really starting to sink in. This was really painful and the one good thing was that Mark didn't know what had happen. He was one of the ones that got Quenton thinking he had something to prove, other than loving his woman. When Quenton got home and laid down in his bed, he could smell Diamond on his pillow, remembering the last time he had slept in this bed she was with him. Tears formed in his eyes, he didn't know he could miss anyone so much.

CHAPTER 13

Fixing Time

Diamond went back to work Marshal and Teresa were the only ones who knew that her heart was broken. She went through the motions with each day getting harder and harder. She missed Quenton so much, but she told herself no more tears, she was a strong woman and wouldn't let anyone break her down. Lost in thought Diamond was planning her trip to New York, wondering how she was going to do what she wanted to do without the guys. "Come on, you promised, Diamond," Curtis said over the phone about coming to the picnic. Diamond dreaded this, got up and went home to change and to go the park where Dennis had planned the first annual Diamond Corporation picnic. Any other time she would have been happy to be there, but this had been the saddest time of her life. But for her father and brother she would try to act like her world had not fallen apart. When Diamond arrived, all of the employees and their families were there. Everyone wanted to speak to Diamond and thank her for their jobs. When she finally got through the crowd of people she went over to where Curtis and Beulah, her parents, were sitting. Also at the table were Cindy and her older sister Lillie and Josie, who Diamond did not know. Lillie's heart was beating hard seeing her daughter. She was so happy but so scared of what her mother would do. Diamond said her hello's to everyone and then started to feel uncomfortable at how this lady kept staring at her. Curtis was telling Diamond how hard Lillie worked at the company. Lillie began to shake knowing that look in her mother's eyes. Josie had been drinking and decided to come to the picnic with Lillie and Cindy, who picked them up. Josie, when she wasn't staring at Diamond, was talking, laughing loudly, cussing, and everyone around her just looked at her. But when she saw Teresa walking with Derrick, her happiness turned to anger. Looking at both of them with hate, she then got up and left. Everyone was happy she was gone, but then she came back with a bottle of beer. Drinking out of the bottle she walked right past Derrick who was so nervous that he was sweating. Josie walked right past him and Teresa, twisting her butt with her too short pants.

Then Teresa smelled it. That smell, it can't be! Trying to hold in her anger, but getting hotter by the minute, said "Josie that's a peculiar fragrance you've got on." "Do you like it? Josie asked. "Not particularly, I just remembered the last time I smelled it, it was on my man's jacket," Teresa replied now steaming. "Well, if you smelled it on your man's jacket, he might not be your man," Josie laughed. "You tramp, how could you stoop so low, I'm your sister!" Teresa yelled. Now at this time Diamond and all those around were listening. Derrick was standing there thinking how to get out of this, glanced at Diamond who was giving him a look he didn't like. Lillie was scared that her mother was going to lose it on her aunt. "Please spare us the drama, Teresa, I don't owe you shit. Standing over there like you're so hurt, you had everything all of your life, everything, even mama's love. And you made her kick me out of the house to care for all of these brats by myself!" Josie yelled back. Cindy and Lillie were looking at each other embarrassed and hurt. "You never took care of anybody but yourself. Lillie raised all of those kids, why all you did was screw any man that came your way and it looks like you're still at it!" Teresa said. She was now in tears and looking at Derrick. Diamond was listening but looked at Lillie and saw how she was suffering in pain at how her mother was behaving. "So what you gonna do about it," Josie yelled. ("No mama") "Lillie was saying to herself "you want to hurt me." ("No mama") you hurt me you hurt Lillie." ("No mama") and if you hurt Lillie, ("No mama") you'll be hurting Diamond's mother, ("Mama No!") Lillie kept saying in her head. "Yes you heard me right my daughter is Diamond's mother!" Josie proudly said. At this time the whole park was mute, not saying a word. They were all looking at Diamond who was staring into Lillie's eyes, and Lillie was thinking about how to help Diamond, who was shaking and looking at her. "No, this scared, weak woman can't be my mother, she's nothing like me," Diamond said to herself and walked away from this madness with Curtis and Beulah following behind her knowing it had to be true, because they looked so much a like, and Curtis finally figuring out why Lillie lots of times reminded him of his daughter. Josie stood there thinking she had accomplished something, watched as all of the people were looking at her in shame. "This time you went too far," Teresa said. Also knowing now why when she looked at Lillie, it made her think of Diamond and also why she felt so close to her. She was her niece's daughter, but she had to leave before she hurt Josie, while Derrick followed behind trying to explain. "Go all of you. I don't need any of you," Josie yelled. Cindy watched Lillie as she sat there like a scared child, shaking just like Diamond. She went up to her mother and said "Mama I don't recall being inside of you knocking on your womb to get out just too screw up your life. For once accept some responsibility for what you do, look at what you did to Lillie," and then Cindy left. Josie looked at Lillie and she was used to seeing her scared, but this sadness that was on her face was too much for even her to bear. She yelled "screw all of you!" and left leaving Lillie sitting there by herself, still shaking unable to move. Curtis and Beulah went over to Diamond and told her to look at Lillie. "I know you consider us your parents and we are, but that scared woman over there is your mother," Beulah said. Then Curtis said "Baby I know Lillie and for her to leave you, it must have been a good reason, because she doesn't have a mean bone in her body." Diamond looked again at this timid woman who was so thin, her clothes were old and she looked like she had been living a hard life. That had Diamond feeling sad for her and hatred for the woman that made Lillie into what she was. Diamond walked over to Lillie who had tears running down her face and asked her if she would come go with her, because they needed to talk. Lillie always wished the day would come that she could spend time with her daughter, but didn't think it would ever come, she got up and followed behind Diamond walking so slowly that Diamond had to slow down so Lillie could keep up with her.

Diamond decided to take Lillie to her house so they could talk. When they got to the house Diamond noticed how Lillie was not in awe of the big mansion she didn't express any emotions at all of the fancy things in the house, and didn't seem to be impressed with any of the material things. Diamond didn't realize that Lillie was a simple woman, never having much and sometimes during her life she didn't even have food, never had new clothes and usually had someone's hand me downs or purchased items at the Goodwill store. That was her way of life and she was used to it. The only thing she desired was to spend time with Diamond. After trying to have a conversation with Lillie, who never said too much, Diamond cooked them both dinners since Josie had made sure a lot of people didn't get to eat at the picnic by running them off. Diamond watched in horror at how Lillie ate a couple of spoonfuls of food and was done. Diamond was ready to bust inside looking at this frail woman and thinking how it looked like she was slowly starving herself to death. Diamond had to get up and walk away so she could pull herself together. After dinner they both sat on the couch and Diamond talked and talked about her life and businesses while Lillie just smiled. She could not comprehend some of the things Diamond talked about. She was just glad to hear her voice and to be able to look in her eyes. Finally in a low whisper Lillie said, "I didn't mean to leave you, I loved you the first time I saw you, but I couldn't take you home to live in that house with Mama. Beulah and Curtis are very good people." After all of these years after finding out she was adopted, Diamond wondered why her parents didn't want her. She was ready to break down at hearing how this woman loved her so much that she gave her up to have a better life than she had. It was so heart wrenching and so unselfish. Not wanting to stop Lillie from opening up took all of Diamond's strength to get her self together and ask about her father. Lillie shook her head no in a way that told Diamond this subject would have to come up later. The ladies were bonding and relaxing around each other so much to where Diamond opened up to Lillie about Quenton. That was the last straw that broke the bridge.

Diamond's emotions were now out of control and she broke down harder than she ever had. The pain and loss of missing Quenton and just meeting her mother overcame her completely. Lillie instantly did what good mother's do. She took her daughter in her arms and held her tight; rocking her back and forth, while Diamond unloaded her grief. Later Diamond asked Lillie to stay with her for a while, so that night as Diamond laid in her bed thinking of all of the things that happened today, she couldn't sleep and decided to go see if Lillie was okay. When she walked over to the room next to her bedroom and slowly opened the door, she saw Lillie sleeping peacefully. Diamond walked over and sat down on the edge of the bed just looking at this woman, saying, "I wonder what kind of life you had. I can sense that you have gone through a lot of things that were not good, and for so many years I thought of how I didn't need you, but it's you that needed me. But don't worry mama, because I'm here for you now." Diamond said then moved the hair out of her mother's face and took her hand and rubbed it for hours just staring at this lonely, scared woman. Diamond couldn't get herself to leave so she laid down beside her mother still holding her hand, scared to let go or leave and she would be gone, she then went to sleep.

Meanwhile back in California the whole family was sad for Quenton. He was a broken man, spending the last few days walking around like a lost sheep. Even his girls were worried about how he was hurting. Chantel asked Tasha how come daddy was acting so strange. Tasha told her sister it was a grownup thing, but deep down she couldn't understand either, for all those years watching her father being sad and lonely to finally find a woman who was so special to him and everyone else, and now to let her go didn't make sense. "Daddy, can I talk to you?" Tasha asked as Quenton sat on the couch letting the TV watch him. "Sure Tasha," he said trying to sound like he was okay. "I don't understand mostly what's going on between you and Diamond, but from what Aunt Laura told me, it has something to do with Diamond being so successful and I'm wondering why, instead of making her suffer behind this, you should be proud of her and what she has accomplished. Daddy, no disrespect, but you were going to marry her when you didn't know she had anything, you planned to help take care of her, but when you find out that she can help you, you can't take it. That's not fair to her and it's not fair to you to lose someone you love so much." Quenton looked at his little girl and watched her turn into a young woman before his eyes. He hugged her as Chantel came in and huddled with them. "You girls love her don't you," Quenton asked his daughters. Both of them shook their heads, yes. "Then I've got to get her back." He finally realized that by pushing Diamond out of his life, he was pushing out the closest thing these girls had as a mother. He was so deep into not being judged by people that he forgot about the ones that really mattered, Tasha, Chantel and also Diamond.

The next few days went by with Lillie staying with Diamond and the two of them bonding. It was a joy to hear Lillie laugh and to see her smile. If Diamond hadn't broken up with Quenton, her life would have been complete. And now getting ready for her trip to New York, Diamond was nervous about coming face to face with Quenton. Terry had called to see if she still needed them to help her out on this mission. Diamond said yes, but deep down she knew what had to be done, and she really wanted to see Quenton again. She had also promised herself that she wouldn't let on how bad she had been missing him. Before Diamond left she told Lillie that she could stay as long as she wanted and that she would be back in a week. Lillie in her quiet voice said to Diamond that she hoped she find what she was looking for and to remember that "true love doesn't come around often and some people never find it, people like me. I can tell you really love that man so fight for him." "Look at my mama talk about fighting for something," Diamond said to herself, but hoped that she would fight the hold Josie had on her.

Later sitting in the elegant Presidential Suite in one of the most exclusive hotels in New York, the three brothers were enjoying the scenery. The suite had a huge living and dining room with three bedrooms. Two were mid size and one was large. Quenton saw the three rooms and put his luggage in the largest one and hoped that when Diamond got there, she would let him stay in there with her. "Man this is living, I can grow to love this" Quincy said. "Don't embarrass us Q, this isn't a vacation it's a job. Something that I know is strange for you but Diamond is counting on us to help her," Quenton told him. "True, in fact I don't plan on letting sis down, but let's be real. Your real reason for being here is to get your woman back and if you don't blow it, maybe you can," Quincy said. "How?" Quenton asked, ready to take any advice he could get, even from Q. "Don't talk, just listen, they eat that shit up. Women think you're being sensitive and caring when what you really care about is keeping them happy, so they can keep you happy. So shut up, let her talk, then get her ass in the bedroom and let that do your talking." Quenton thought some of that stuff Q said made sense. While waiting for Diamond's arrival, Quenton was so nervous he kept getting up looking out the window. "Man, sit down. If she got you that sprung you shouldn't have ever let her go in the first place!" Quincy said. Then he and Quenton began arguing about what Quincy said when Diamond walked in she had on a beautiful short black dress, she wore her hair down and her makeup was perfect. Diamond wanted to show Quenton what he was passing up. "Hey lady, you're looking nice," Terry said. "No sis, you are fine," Quincy threw in. Quenton was speechless upon seeing her and it really hit home how much he missed her. Just looking at her he wanted to grab her and rush her into the bedroom. "Hello everyone," Diamond said trying not to make eye contact with Quenton who was staring her down. Diamond sat down and talked to the fellows and told them what she wanted done. Terry and Quenton listened carefully, knowing their jobs were to go over the books and Quenton's specialty, getting the plant to run efficiently. Quincy was to go in with Diamond as new hires. Diamond had one inside man, one of the managers that had it set up for them to come in to work. After talking about what time to meet at the plant Terry asked Diamond if she would join them for dinner and where was her luggage. Quenton was waiting to hear, hoping he wouldn't have to bunk with one of his brothers, but was sad to hear that she had her own room on the third floor, one of the smaller rooms. "You don't have to do that baby, I mean Diamond, there's that big room. I have my stuff in it for now," hoping she would say leave it and stay with him. He was let down when she told him that was okay as she was already settled. "So what about dinner?" Quenton asked sadly. "I'm going to go to the dining area below and get me a bite to eat, thank you anyway," she said, then got up and left.

"Pit-i-ful, man you better go see about your woman, you can't let her go down there by herself looking like that!" Quincy said.

Quenton thought about it and he knew some dude would try to pick up his woman, he gave Q a pound and left. Diamond laughed to herself as she saw Quenton sitting at the bar trying not to act like he wasn't there for her. He hoped she would come over to him and let him make up to her. After eating Diamond got up and made a point to swish her hips, she knew it turned him on and walked up to Quenton and asked him if he wanted her to buy him a drink. He smiled and asked "you trying to pick me up?" "No." No? he thought. "I just thought you might want a drink and to tell you that I'm going to my room, so you can stop stalking me." "It's called protecting and that's different, Diamond!" Quenton said getting upset. He then walked her to her room, both of them not saying anything, but Quenton was hoping she would invite him in, but was shut down again, when she said goodbye and closed the door. Diamond wanted to yank Quenton in that room and make passionate love to him. It wasn't fair for him to open that door of love making, and then close it on her. If he really wanted her, he would have to prove it. She was determined to not get let down again.

The next morning everyone left for work. Quenton and Terry in a limo, and Quincy and Diamond on a bus. "This don't make no sense, I hear you own a plane and we're riding a bus," Quincy complained to Diamond. "Stop complaining Q this is what working people do." "That's one of the hundred other reasons I don't work," Quincy stated. When they got to the plant it was a huge building and in front of the building it had a sign on it, Diamond Corporation. Quincy laughed saying "it would be funny if you got fired on the first day at your own company." Diamond told him that she would be amazed if he made it through the week. To make it not seem like a set up, the inside man had ten new hires along with Diamond and Quincy. The first thing Diamond noticed was how unfriendly some of the people were. Diamond didn't like how she and the other people were greeted. They were taken to a room and waited for their supervisor. A short black woman named Mrs. Collins, came in and told the workers what they were to do. Then she got rude, saying that if they didn't cut it, she would fire them in a second. Diamond was on fire listening to this woman.

Quincy was placed on the other side of the factory. Diamond was placed on an assembly line with two other women, a black woman of medium build with dark skin and short hair named Alisha, the other lady was a small Hispanic woman named Grazelda. Right away they began to show 'Diane' what to do, being that Mrs. Collins didn't. Strike two, Diamond thought. She caught on quick, which impressed the two ladies and they asked her to join then for lunch. Diamond, who was going under the name of Diane, started asking about the place. Grazelda wasn't going to talk too much, she was afraid of losing her job. Alisha, on the other hand, let it go. She told Diamond how they got talked to rudely, having their breaks shortened, made to stay longer, but not getting paid. That meant if they had an order to get out at quitting time, they had to stay and do it, only getting paid for eight hours. Sometimes they worked up to an hour over and were not told ahead if they were to stay late. So if you had kids at the sitter or at school, you would be late to pick them up. The money wasn't right, the vacation was only one week, even if you had been there for over three years and it took that long to get it. But the worse was Mrs. Collins and how rude and unfair she was to everyone. Diamond disgusted with herself that her plant was being run like this. Even though she had a lot of plants and she couldn't see all of the problems they had, but something this wrong should have come to her attention earlier, other than by an employee that wanted to be nameless. Diamond figured it was Alisha. "You know, I wrote the owners of this plant a letter and they don't even give a damn," Alisha yelled. Diamond was saying to herself, "yes I do, and first I'm going to change the atmosphere of the plant. She looked at the lunchroom that had nothing but a few tables and a small refrigerator and one microwave available. People were forced to eat cold food because they all couldn't get to the microwave before lunch was over. The place was dark and gloomy and didn't have enough chairs. Some people had to stand to eat or worse, sit on the floor. That was tearing her up. When Quincy joined the ladies at the table he brought with him a tall, dark, slender man with a process and a mustache named Tony. He sat down and immediately started trying to get next to Diamond. "What's your name pretty lady?" "My name is Diane," and then she introduced Quincy to the ladies as her brother. Everyone was talking when one of the managers brought Terry and Quenton over. They were in their business suits, looking fine. Diamond was smiling at Quenton and he at her until he noticed this man trying to whisper in her ear. Quincy was trying to hold back the laughter, because he knew that look Quenton was giving. The manager introduced Terry and Quenton as visitors that would be looking around checking out the plant. Everyone went back to work when Diamond noticed she didn't see Mrs. Collins and there were a lot of people that were not working. Since there was no one there to tell them what to do, they sat down on boxes, and talked with other workers who kept leaving the area of work. Diamond was steaming, but she knew now why they weren't making any money. People were not pulling their own weight, while others like Alisha and Grazelda had to work harder. About an hour before closing, here comes Mrs. Collins and a younger black man. "That's her son Billy. Notice how he's just getting to work, but ends up with the same amount of pay as us. And look at her, see how she left with one hair style and comes back with another," Alisha said. Strike three, when the day was over and Diamond and Quincy were waiting at the bus stop, with Quincy complaining that Tony said he was going to give them a ride, but Diamond didn't want him to think he had any action coming from her. Then Alisha and her father, who was driving an old beat up truck, offered them a ride. Quincy looked at Diamond with an oh no you don't look. Diamond smiled and got in the front seat with Alisha and her father while Quincy sat outside in the back mumbling. Then they dropped them off a block away from the hotel Diamond offered to pay them for the ride, but they wouldn't take it and Alisha's father said they could pick them up in the morning to take them to work for free and that he was just glad to be able to help. Diamond told Quincy "See, that's what I'm talking about." "That's because you ain't got to sit in the back," he complained some more.

The group got together to discuss the first day. Diamond came in wearing a satin outfit looking sexy. Quenton thought she could at least not try to turn him on with her sexy outfits. After Terry and Quenton told Diamond that there was a lot of mismanagement with the money. Quenton expressed how they had determined how certain items they ran were costly. Quincy told the group that the workers were saying the same thing Alisha said about the treatment. "Well, for our first mission Terry I want two big new refrigerators, and four new microwaves. I want new tables and chairs to accommodate everyone and I need the lunch room painted in bright colors and bring in a lounging couch and TV so people can relax at breaks and lunch. "When do you need this done," Quenton asked. "Let's start tomorrow. Thank you and goodnight," she said, and then left to go to her room. Diamond noticed how Quenton followed her making sure she got to her room, and then she could hear him cuss when she closed the door. The next day went like the other, except for the people coming in to fix up the lunchroom. Diamond noticed this was the second day and Grazelda wasn't eating, so she offered some of her lunch to her but she refused. Diamond couldn't stand to watch people hungry, which made her think of Lillie.

Lillie had been going to work and then going back to Diamond's home. Josie finally decided to come home after staying a few nights with this gangster named Blue, she then found out Lillie was gone. Josie called around to Cindy and if she knew, she wasn't going to tell her anyway. She then called Derrick who was furious. "You lost me my job bitch; I thought you were going to give me the top spot. When I went to work on Monday I got a pink slip and now Teresa won't even answer my calls!" he cussed at her. "Look, I told you I was going to get it for you. I will. You saw how Diamond was looking at Lillie, you help me find my daughter and I'll hook you up," Josie said. "I'll look around, but this better work," he said. "Don't worry, I got me some help now" she said.

"Quincy I need some money," Diamond stated. "What, you need some what, sis you must be joking." "No seriously, Alisha told me Grazelda doesn't have any money for lunch or food at home. I want to put some money in her bag." Quincy looked in his wallet and pulled out a twenty-dollar bill. "Oh hell no, you stingy man," Diamond said then yanked his wallet out of his hand and took two hundred dollars and put it in her bag. Quincy just stood there shaking his head. "Grazelda will thank you," Diamond said. "Hey, Grazelda better be happy because I usually get more than a thank you when I give a woman that kind of money," he said. After getting home Grazelda found the money in her bag and was so happy, knowing it was one of her coworkers and decided to make lunch for everyone. Diamond felt good helping good people like Grazelda who worked hard and was always lending a hand to help anyone. Quincy was feeling good about what Diamond did and was hoping that his brother could somehow get her back, and then a light bulb went off in his head. He smiled to himself and asked Tony about the nightspots and how he would like to go to one of them. Then here it comes, "I'll show you if you hook me up with your sister," Tony smiled. Quincy smiled back and said, "I'll ask her." Part one of the plan was started. He then told Diamond that he had asked Alisha out and that he wanted her to come out with them. She declined, but after pleading, Diamond said she would but she wasn't going to stay out late. He didn't mention to her that Tony was coming. "Quenton, Tony's trying to take Diamond out tonight." Part two was initiated. "What!" Quenton yelled. You could see the veins popping out of his neck, but that wasn't nothing. When he saw Diamond walk in the room with this short, tight, low cut red dress on, with her hair and makeup done, Quenton was ready to burst. Just thinking about a man trying to go where no other man had been before was sending him to the roof. While they sat there going over the day's projects, Quenton was looking at Diamond angrily. Diamond was wondering why he was glaring at her like that. "Oh, he's jealous that I'm going out, how cute," and it was turning her on. After the meeting Diamond got up to go and the dress was so short that Quenton noticed the look on his brother's faces. Diamond was showing too much leg. "Where do you think you're going?" Quenton demanded. "I'm going out." "Out where and with whom and why?" "I think I'm over eighteen and I can do what I want without having to answer all of these questions." "Well, it looks like you want to get picked up, maybe from that dude at the job that's been whispering in your ear and following you all around!" Quenton yelled. "Well, if I did want to get picked up at least he wouldn't make me sign nothing," she yelled back. "Oh hell no," Quenton thought, she's referring to the prenup. Terry and Quincy observing with their eyes and mouth open knew it was on. Quenton and Diamond started yelling at each other. Quincy, trying to help, said "both of you ought to go to the bedroom and relieve all of that stress, yeah, go sweat off all of that hostility." Both Diamond and Quenton turned their heads at the same time and said, "Shut up Quincy!" and continued to argue. "If you need a chip knocked off, I can do that for you, you ain't got to go to old dude!" Quenton yelled. "Wait a minute, don't you care what people will say. Because people say I should move on and find someone else, should I listen," Diamond shot back, silencing Quenton who was now getting the point. Diamond had brought it to his attention how wrong he was for letting people make him feel like he had to please them, she had flipped the script. He stood there shaken, and then walked into the bedroom and closed the door knowing that he had made a mistake and had lost a love that could never be replaced. Sitting on the bed in the dark room, he heard a knock on the door. "I don't feel like talking." Thinking it was one of his brothers. "I don't feel like talking either," Diamond said as she walked into the room and into his open arms. They stood there just holding each other for awhile until Diamond said, "I do need a chip knocked off, can you help me." Quenton barely able to restrain him self, told her to get in that bed and set the alarm because it's going to be a long night. Afterwards as they lay in each other's arms, Quenton told Diamond that he loved her so much and that he wanted to wake up every morning and to go bed every night with her. "What are you saying, or you asking me to marry you?" Diamond asked. "Yes I am, just me," he said. "What about the prenup?" Diamond dreaded to ask. "Only if you want one," he said. Diamond looked Quenton in his eyes and told him. "I do not. Our marriage is going to last forever. When I say I do, it's not until later or just for now, it means I do forever. I'm in it for the long haul, can you handle that," Diamond asked him. Quenton smiled and told her "if you can handle that, the last eyes I want to see before I close mine for the last time are yours." Diamond kissed him and told him that she felt the same way and that she couldn't wait to tell her mother. Then she told Quenton about Lillie, and just thinking about her Diamond began to get misty. When Quenton heard this it made him love her more seeing that she really did need him, not in a financial way but in a physical and emotional way. "I got you, I got you baby," he told her and then they both fell asleep holding each other.

CHAPTER 14

Enough!

"There she is, get her Blue!" Josie yelled. Then Blue grabbed Lillie from the bus stop and yanked her into the car with Josie and Derrick, who was driving the car and thinking this, is getting a little out of hand. Lillie was shaking. "Where's Diamond?" Josie asked. Lillie was scared but not that scared to let them hurt her daughter. She just looked at her mother, and then Josie slapped her across the face. "Okay, you want to act like that, we'll make her come to us," Josie stated then they drove off.

When Diamond walked in the lunchroom she saw that it was fully decorated and had hot and cold machines and she saw Mrs. Collins and her son sitting on the couch eating and watching TV. When Mrs. Collins saw her she asked Diamond what she was doing in there and to get back to work. Diamond gave her a look, then bit her lip and turned around and made it to the door, then said to herself "Oh hell no!" She turned around and went over and told Mrs. Collins she was a bad example for the workers to see. "No, what I am is the HNIC up in here and you won't have to look at me anymore, you're fired!"

"Fired!" Now back at the hotel, "you mean I made it longer than you," Quincy was roaring. Diamond was more embarrassed watching Quincy laughing at her. She went on to say that "Mrs. Collins had the nerve to tell me she was the HNIC." "She said that to you," Quincy said now laughing so hard he had tears in his eyes. Terry did not understand what was so funny asked, "What does HNIC mean?" Quincy was looking at Terry like he was an alien from another planet. "Terry, you are the whitest black man I know. You don't know nothing HNIC means Head Nigga in Charge." "That bit of information I can do without knowing, and I'm surprised you know that, because being in charge has to do with work, and we all know you're not very familiar with that," Terry shot back. "Well at least I didn't get fired," Quincy laughed again at Diamond. Quenton was not amused by any of this and told the group it was time to end this.

The next morning there was a plant meeting called. Everyone was there, all of the employees, managers and supervisors. Quenton and Terry were on the platform with one of the managers who told the workers that they had a special guest. Then Diamond walked to the platform and introduced herself as Diamond Bradford, owner of the Diamond Corporation. Diamond stated some knew her as Diane, and that she and her team, pointing at Quenton Terry and now Quincy on stage. "We came to the plant undercover to see some of the problems here, and because someone," now looking at Alisha and Grazelda who were shocked, "cared enough to call me to help. The lunchroom was the first step to improve the working environment here. There's more, we will be issuing out raises according to ability and you will be paid for every minute you work. You'll be getting vacation up to five weeks, depending on years worked. My team has come up with ideas that will save lots of revenue with just good planning. Now we will be passing out bonuses for my appreciation and my apology for what some of you have been going through. Some of you will be getting a little more in your envelopes, pink slips," and Diamond looked at Mrs. Collins. Her mouth was open so wide you could get a bus through it. "Now take rest of the day off with pay. Thank you." Everyone was standing up and clapping and Diamond's team was feeling so proud and happy of what they had done. Diamond was so impressed with Quenton and Terry and how they worked out a plan and strategy to help the plant. Alisha walked over to Diamond feeling ashamed. "Ooh girl, the things I said about your company will you please forgive me." "Don't worry because I've got plans for you and Grazelda," Diamond said and appointed them both supervisors and when Alisha and her father got home, they had a brand new truck parked in their driveway, complements of the Diamond Corporation.

Flying back home on her private plane, along with Quenton, Quincy and Terry, Diamond told them all how proud she was of them and the good job they had done. She was looking forward to them taking over all of the company's business with Quenton as the CEO. Quenton humbled thinking she just put a multi million dollar company in my lap, what could top that. "Then what will you do?" Terry asked. Diamond looked at Quenton and smiled and said "I'll just stay home and have babies." That was it, the topper. Quenton took Diamond in his arms. "I can't wait to extend our family but we have to get married first." Diamond arrived home ready to tell Lillie, Curtis, Beulah and Teresa of her marriage plans, when she got a message on her phone that Lillie wanted her to come to this address from Josie. Diamond thinking that Lillie had went back home, so she decided to go get her from the clutches of Josie. Diamond didn't know if it would work, since Josie had Lillie for so long.

When Diamond got to the house and walked in, there was Lillie sitting on the couch with Josie standing over her and Derrick stood next to her. This did not look good Diamond was then pushed, from behind by this big black man. Josie kept calling Blue. Diamond was trying to act like she wasn't scared. "What's going on, why do you have my mother here?" "She lives here," Josie said coldly. "What do you want lady, since you tricked me here?" Diamond asked. Josie walked over to Diamond, with Lillie now even more afraid for her daughter. "Look Diamond, since my daughter brought you into this world and I brought her, I feel that I'm entitled to some of those millions you got." "Lady, I don't know you, I've never known you and don't want to know you. What I do know is that you're the one that hurt my mother and got her scared to live. You had her so scared that she couldn't even bring me home around you because she knows you're evil," Diamond told her. Josie upset at what Diamond had said to her slapped Diamond hard on the side of her face. Diamond just stood there, but Lillie's fear turned to anger. "Look, I could have given my kids away like Lillie, but I chose to keep them," Josie yelled. "That wasn't an act of love because if you did love them, you would have let them get raised up by good people and have good lives. Lady, you kept them to make their lives as horrible as yours," Diamond yelled back. "Why you little bitch," Josie yelled then went to slap Diamond again when "Enough!" Lillie yelled. She jumped up and caught Josie's wrist looking her straight in her eyes, and with a powerful voice said "Enough mama!" You beat me, you beat my brother's and sister's, but I won't let you ever beat my daughter!" Lillie was yelling at Josie who was now the scared woman. This was the first time seeing her daughter angry and ready to protect her child like a mother lion would her cub. Diamond was standing behind her mother, now knowing where her strength had come from. Lillie had it; it just had to be brought out, by something that she loved more than her own life, her daughter. "Look, you bitches can have your family feud later. I came here to get paid Josie!" Blue yelled and pulled out a gun. Derrick, upon seeing the gun, ran out the house like the coward he was. "Oh wait," Josie said, frightened that this was getting out of hand. "We don't need to go there Blue, we were just supposed to scare them like I told you to do to Lewis, the man that raped Lillie," (Mama was raped, oh no, how wonder mama didn't want to talk about my father he raped her, Diamond thought). "Josie, why do you think you haven't seen Lewis for so many years and will never see him, because I don't play, he's fish food," Blue told her. Josie was very scared for both Lillie and Diamond, after hearing that Blue had killed Lewis, knew she had to do something quick. She slowly walked up to Blue, smiling, talking about how she was going to make sure he got paid and when she got close enough, she grabbed for the gun with all of her might and tried to get the gun from Blue until, Blam! The gun went off with the bullet hitting Josie in the chest. Josie fell down on the floor. "Mama!" Lillie yelled, and then knelt down at her side. Josie was stinging from the pain and slowly losing her air, told Lillie "baby I'm so sorry for all of the pain I took you through. I did love you, always have. I just needed someone to hurt like me. Stop now, stop hurting and go live," and she was gone. "Mama, no, mama," Lillie cried. Diamond was hurting for her mother, but still watched Blue as he pointed the gun at her. "Look lady, you're next if you don't get me my money!" "No!" Lillie yelled, seeing Blue pointing the gun at Diamond, jumped up to grab the gun. Bang!

Five years later, Diamond was sitting on the couch at the mansion with her husband Quenton, who just got home from the office. Diamond was thinking that now after all of her success and trials, she was now finally able to sit back and let her husband and his brother Terry, along with Marshal and Teresa, take care of the company. Felisha now owned the store she had previously worked at and came out with her own clothing line. The kids were in school and Tasha was attending college majoring in business. Dennis still ran the plant while Curtis was retired and relaxing at home with Beulah. The Walker's new restaurant was up and running. Quincy replaced Mark as lead singer and Laura Lee and he were on tour singing around the world, still arguing, but only flying now. As a present from Quenton and Diamond, Joe was living at the Walker's in his tour bus. Diamond was thinking how everyone was doing good when four-year old Quenton Jr. ran in the house and jumped into his parent's laps. He was followed by a new and improved Lillie now with meat on her bones, she was all done up in a beautiful peach colored dress, high heels and her hair was cut in a short sassy style and her makeup was expertly applied. "Hello family," she said with volume and confidence. I brought somebody back to you and now I've got to go. I've got a nice gentleman waiting for me outside in his car." Diamond smiled and asked, "Where are you going mama?" "To live baby, to live," Lillie smiled and walked out.

THE END BY JANETTE A RUCKER 9-20-2007.

ABOUT THE AUTHOR

My name is Janette A Rucker and I just hit the big 50 and I've been blessed to have grown up with two wonderful parents my father Robert Andrews Sr. is now gone to glory but was the best father a child/adult could ask for. My mother Janette Andrews is a beautiful exciting spicy woman (I won't tell her age) but she looks good!" "That's my mama!"

My husband Robert Lee Rucker is my prince and my rock that I have been married to for over twenty five years. And my life for the most part has been good, but at the darkest time of my life I started writing and it got me through and after the first two novels I couldn't stop. My prayer is that I touch someone's heart and tell them how good God is in every situation but I do at times "go there" because I want to keep it real and make you laugh at the same time. So hopefully you will enjoy this book and the others to come.

Thanks peace and love

Janette A Rucker.